As You Desire Me

Fiona Cooper

by the same author:
Rotary Spokes
Heartbreak on the High Sierra
Not the Swiss Family Robinson
Jay Loves Lucy
The Empress of the Seven Oceans
A Skyhook in the Midnight Sun
Blossom at the Mention of Your Name

I Believe in Angels
(short-story collection)

First published 2004 by Red Hot Diva/Diva Books,
an imprint of Millivres Prowler Limited
Spectrum House, Unit M, 32–34 Gordon House Road, London NW5 1LP
www.divamag.co.uk

A catalogue record for this book is available from the British Library

ISBN 1-873741-92-8

Printed and bound in Finland by WS Bookwell

Distributed in the UK and Europe by Airlift Book Company,
8 The Arena, Mollison Avenue,
Enfield, Middlesex EN3 7NJ
Telephone: 020 8804 0400

Distributed in North America by Consortium,
1045 Westgate Drive, St Paul, MN 55114-1065
Telephone: 1 800 283 3572

Distributed in Australia by Bulldog Books,
PO Box 300, Beaconsfield, NSW 2014

"Your heart's desires be with you!"

William Shakespeare

Call me Alex.

All through the basement years, sex was cheaper than free and alcohol gushed like a wildcat oil strike. Most sunrises found me snow-blind and evening shadows coated the city streets like fallout. Every night I just wanted to get up and get out of my head. So, I did. In smoky cellars, strobe-crazy clubs, tequila kitchens and alien bathrooms. Over and over I found that love cost more than money; hell, love was just a four-letter word in the basement years and when I was looking for proof – well, there it was, all 40% of it, running through my weary veins and making a smokescreen of my head.

It was life, I guess, and then one day I woke up with another less than perfect stranger in the bed beside me and a volcanic cloud in my head. Looking at the soot-streaked window with its top six inches of half light, waiting for the kettle to boil – with a fierce urgency it all ceased to be life as I wished to know it.

I left my basement for a place where the rooms had windows and the sun came through and I traded my dungarees for navy blue and white and took a chance on the nine to five.

I did office stuff and rose to the dizzy heights of office manager and god, was I efficient and fair. I got the Employee of the Year Award. A dead-eyed lady with a lipstick smile stood shaking my hand and everything went in slow motion. Jesus! She was me in ten years if I stuck to that road and I knew I had to go. It was a gut feeling that rose to my throat like suppressed laughter – or a scream.

After that, I'd fallen for Jodie in a big way, and she lived in Glastonbury where you look out of the window and see trees. Yeah, Jodie lived with Martin, a husband she managed to ignore often enough to have me believe in us as a future. The executive wardrobe I lost to the Red Cross shop and I hippied it out under Joanna's wing. But you get tired of being in the wings, no matter how wonderful and breathy the words and the sex. It was eighteen months down the line that I realised I'd always be Martin's understudy. My get-up-and-go kicked me in the gut and filled my mouth with salt tears and Oxfam gained three bags full of tie dye and Indian cotton.

I found a nice lap dancer called Randy in LA, and a few years as a courier. Spain was Suzie the belly dancer who had a way with baby oil; Kuwait was Latisha the painter who had to fuck face down; Amsterdam was Marijke, Kristin, Elena or any combination of the three; Sardinia was Lady X, the fur fetishist who only came alive at moonrise; Hawaii was Madame, and Madame was into everything. She nicknamed me the Flying Fuck, which I took as a compliment.

Hustlers and *les riches* – nouveaux and old. The money bought a lot of fun.

On a balcony in Capri, talking to the Marquesa, a Botox-and-silicone-enhanced squanderer whose tan lay taut on her skin, that *gotta go* feeling came again. This time, I had good enough threads to be worth selling, and back in London, I did burglar alarms for a while until I notched up a record number of sales for four months in a row, and after the flashbulbs and hand-shaking, I disappeared to an all-night burger bar called El Dorado. That was Sheila, the manageress, fifty-ish, divorced and henna-ed. Sheila was fine until she got too intimate with General Gordon and his bottle-green misery water.

One night, a bunch of theatre dykes came in to El Dorado, Sheila was passed out by the fryer, and I gave my phone number to Shelley, a set designer. Cleaning up for the morning shift, sobering Sheila up, hearing her ramble about the way I was after her job for the boringth time, I knew that was my last day of maroon polyester dungarees, and that even a charity shop wouldn't want the check shirt – nothing could shift the deep-fried aftertang of the El Dorado.

After that, it was play posters and Shelley, until I was in demand and the phone rang mainly for me. And Shelley got jealous and I got restless and late post-theatre sleepless nights brought rage and melodrama and had my guts churning and my feet itching.

Then I found myself a nice girl, and thought maybe mellow and an absence of drama meant it was the real thing. Until seven years on and the night our friends started talking about what an example we were to everyone, an example of a relationship that lasted, and I listened and went *uh huh*, knowing that we had become a non-sexual domestic habit, and there was no spark, still less the magical flicker of flame, and I thought of all the affairs and one-night stands I was wanting to have. So I binned all the sensible shoes and practical outfits and headed out of London and knew that I would never go back again.

This time I used every contact in my phone book, swearing that I'd decide where I was going and what I was doing next, rather than following the blind foolishness of my heart.

So now I do houses.

Tell me what you want and I do it.

My words and sketches flesh out your dreams. A semi or a terrace or a mansion, it's your palace and by the time you sign a contract with me, you know you're stepping into dreamland.

When things are slack with fixtures and fittings, I pour resin into moulds and make bronze-effect heads of the dead and famous. Churchill, Einstein, Beethoven, Mozart, Elvis. You buy them to add a touch of class to your living space. I do chess sets too, Chinese emperors and samurai pawns, King Arthur and Captain Kirk, with

Merlin and Mr Spock as bishops.

Hell, I'm adaptable.

I have a way of blending with you – if you yearn for a quarry-tiled kitchen with a reclaimed and beeswaxed farmhouse table, dried flowers, hand-turned spice rack, mother-earth colours and an Aga at the heart of your home, then you'll remember me in russets and leaf green, my cheeks glowing with health, raring for country walks, talking wholesome soups and blackberrying.

Or you. Take me into your living room, gleaming with neo-Bauhaus discomfort. My words sparkle like the collection of empty bottles you will pay a fortune for. Picture me in black and white and funereal mauve. You will forever see my white scarf draped across the tubular steel of your favourite chair.

And you? Oh, you deco darling! The crook of my finger shadows the delicate handle of your repro Clarice Cliff cups. My shirt is a Klimt tapestry, my eyes are curved blue glass. My laughter makes your clear goblets ring, my hands paint holograms as I speak, shimmering like your crystal chandeliers.

You will never have felt at ease the way you do with me. Sure, you have combed IKEA and Habitat, walked the dawn at antique fairs and flea markets, assembling your props. I find the missing jigsaw piece, I make it all fit and god, do you feel good. Now you are just the way you want to show yourself.

I slide into your milieu as seamlessly as a snake glides into the dark waters round a mangrove root, scarcely a ripple, and I am a creature breathing water as easily as air.

And it's the same with sex.

I slip into waves of your desire as sleek as a seal, I am an acrobat in this bubble-streaked world, and you take my fin as I corkscrew and dive, taking you deeper than you thought possible. Or safe. As deep as your most fantastic dreams. I leave you breathless and dizzy, crazy for more, in a world where safe no longer matters, now all your limits have gone.

Only don't use the L word. Not unless you mean it and I mean it too.

The L word strikes my guts like a savage hook and rips me up and away and I have to vanish through the silver roof of this thrilling ocean. The L word always turns someone – usually me – into a trophy, record-breaking, tarnished and dead.

Leave out the L word and we can take a magic carpet ride.

Leave out the L word and I will belong with you wherever we are.

Few things irritate me. Meanness, I guess. Why hoard money when you can drink champagne or eat lobster? Time enough for beans on toast and tea when money is thin and you're alone. And meanness with sex. That stings like poison dumped in a clear river. Why hold back any part of your body when every cell can take you flying? I'll whirl you on an inter-galactic superhighway of ecstasy.

What are you waiting for?

Just tell me what you want me to do.

The time is right now.

Call me Alex.

I am a chameleon.

One

I was on the train to London for Gay Pride.

This was to be a feel-good weekend, hanging out with Niall, a queen from the El Dorado days, and the brandy I sipped soothed every cell of my body with its instant illusory promise that *everything's gonna be all right!* Brandy is a sweet lying bitch. But somehow I had to get past York without jumping out of the train.

York was where Emilia lived.

Now, I wasn't In Love with Emilia; I had sworn off all that L stuff, but she had me kind of intrigued. I could have been in L with her, but she hadn't given me any sign that's what she wanted, and one-way unrequited is a tune played on a one-stringed guitar. And I didn't see Emilia much, anyway. I don't do one-to-one long distance.

Somehow, when I moved the last time, footloose and fancy free and determined to stay that way, my heart had almost got hooked on Emilia. Self-preservation made me hold back enough of my heart to stay sane. I'd gone to visit Marcie, an old friend who would become an enemy since she happened to be living with Emilia. I guess you can choose where your heart leads you; I've read that it's possible, but the map of my life is zig-zagged with love, In Love at every sharp turn. Besides, Emilia seemed dangerously exciting, tall and blonde and dramatic to the point of tragedy. She spoke to me of love in breathy phone calls; she always arrived late and for only hours at a time, cried for half of those hours about Marcie; she obsessed about her traumatic childhood and told me I was the only one who understood her. It all added up to a cocktail of fascination for me.

I told Niall all about it in late-night phone calls and he was scathingly unsympathetic.

'Darling, you've only just extricated your sanity from those years of Porridge,' he said. 'Why can't you find yourself some pretty pussy to play with and have some fun?'

Porridge was his name for my ex, because, he said, she was wholesome and sensible and good for me. And impossibly dreary.

'Let me feed back to you,' he said. 'This Emilia is attached or semi-detached, depending on her mood. She is addicted to self-dramatisation. She can do phone sex from midnight to four am when you've been working your ass off all day. You are spending all the bank's money on restaurants and flowers and bijou gifties and posh booze and turning your new home into a sparkly love-shrine for her, and she comes to see you once in a while and weeps her heart out...is there something I've missed?'

'I think I might love her,' I said. 'She's a Goddess.'

'Really dear, one is no longer seventeen,' said Niall, sighing. 'Do you know the Moomintroll books? Marvellous! All life is on those pages. There is a creature in there called a Groke who is huge and grey and attracted always to light and heat. In one story she is drawn to a bonfire on the beach, but as she goes towards it, the sand and the sea freeze over and the bonfire becomes grey ash. All the good and happy creatures flee at her approach, for she is the kiss of death. I believe you've found yourself a Groke, darling, not a Goddess. No good will come of it.'

I didn't like thinking of Emilia that way, but as the winter nights became longer and lonelier, I knew he was right. Only, as soon as I withdrew a little from the hopeless frost, Emilia would suddenly flare enough enthusiasm to make my heart lurch from pain to joy.

I had decided, however, that I would not let the cold kill me.

As York station flashed by, I raised my plastic glass to her, Emilia, the Goddess, the Groke, whatever she was, however good or bad she was for me.

I set my mind on the weekend ahead, and even thought I'd ring Porridge and say hey how're you doing? I was so little in London these days it seemed a good idea to be sociable.

Like a school reunion, Pride guarantees enough familiar faces for you to remember who you were pretending to be when you met them, enough music to bring back the screaming nights and tarty days when your act was so perfect that you even swallowed it yourself. Faces from bars, buses and pillows, voices from phone calls and answerphones and sweet-sweet-nothing smooches, bodies from when we were very, very young indeed.

I was walking across the wino-strewn concourse of Kings Cross, dragging my weekend bag, when I was accosted by a smooth-faced man – rather smart, jacket and dress pants and gleaming shoes. Oh, what a thing to tell Niall!

'Can I help you with that?'

The voice gave it away – not a man at all, but one of those ex-Forces dykes who gets her kicks out of being taken for one. Not the type that ever grabs me or gets the juices flowing, but whether it was the brandy or the anarchy of Pride coursing through my veins, I smiled.

'Thank you,' I said.

She took the handle of my bag. 'Where are you going?'

Good god, she was blushing! I fluttered my eyelashes and mentally flipped a coin.

'I have to go to the loo,' I said.

So we walked together, past the tired-faced whores and the queues snaking their refugee weariness. I tried walking like a girl and managed not to laugh when my gallant companion slowed a little and hooked one thumb in her belt.

'I'm Jools,' she said.

'I'm Emily,' I said, before I could think. Well, why not?

And then we were through the heavy doors of the loo, and the disabled door was wide open in front of us. I looked at Jools and smiled.

'Are you coming in with me?' I said.

She stood with her back to me while I peed, her hands thrust into her pockets. I could see her blushing slightly as I studied her square-chinned profile in the mirror. Well, life is full of experiences, so I washed my hands and leaned against the wall.

She turned and her eyes questioned mine. I let my head lean back a little and sure enough, she leaned towards me, one arm on the wall by my shoulder. Her face came close to mine and her mouth nuzzled my mouth, suddenly all tongues when I parted my lips. She pushed me hard against the wall, and her hand clasped my breast, then, shoved up inside my T-shirt, flicking my bra undone in seconds. I put my hands on her waist and she banged her self into me, her other hand parting my thighs and her muscled thigh nudging against my tingling cunt, the hard denim seam almost painful. I tugged her shirt buttons loose and felt the solid flesh of her midriff. Hot and horny.

'You want to do this?' she said.

'What do you think?' I said, grabbing her square ass and digging my fingers in.

'Let me,' she said, tugging at the fly of my jeans and shoving them down to my knees, 'Don't do anything, Emily, let me.'

I kicked my jeans off and smiled at her. 'How do you want me?'

She was breathing hard now, and tugged my T-shirt off, with the bra. The tiles of the wall were icy against my back and she pinned me there with her shoulders, while her hard and hasty hands squeezed my breasts and belly, her thigh still nudging at me like a jackhammer.

'Are you wet for it?' she said, one hand fumbling between my legs.

'You're soaking,' she said, and pushed one finger hard against me, then her tongue fucked my throat while her finger went right inside. Her thumb flicked against my clit and her finger went deeper. Again, almost pain, but not quite.

'Tell me it's good,' she said, sweating against my cheek.

'It's good,' I said, and the hardness and thrust of her hand made my body jerk. 'Jesus, it's good.'

'The best you've had,' she gasped.

'Just keep doing it,' I said. 'It's good; god, it's good.'

Her arm lifted me from the floor and she bore down on me, stretching me full length. My head was right beside the pedestal of the loo, and she stood there, took off her trousers and her boxers and folded them neatly beside her shoes. She buttoned her shirt again and lay on top of me, pushing my thighs wide apart with her body, her arm like a steel bar between her flesh and mine. Her ass heaved and pushed against me, her hand like a prick bruising inside me and she kissed me so deep I was gasping.

'You're a fucking lady,' she said. 'You're a woman.'

'Fuck me, you bastard,' I said suddenly realising where the glazed look in her eyes was taking her. 'You're my man, such a big boy; god, you're the best.'

Now her head rose above me and a vein stood out in her neck. Her ass thumped up and down and I felt myself ready to come with the heat and the wetness her hand was plundering inside me.

'Make me come, Jools,' I gasped, 'make me come.'

'Can you take me?' she said, looking down into my eyes.

'Try me,' I said, 'I want to take all of you.'

Suddenly as she writhed on top of me, I felt a cool smoothness inside me, and a wonderful deep vibration. She fucked like a man, only I knew this was battery-assisted and I pulled the length of the vibrator inside me, then pushed it out against her until we built up the thrust and tug, then faster and faster, and I cried out as the orgasm swept through me. Jools wasn't finished; she straddled my thigh and worked herself against me until she groaned and collapsed, the full dead weight of her on top of me.

My mouth was swamped with sloppy kisses and then she sat up, and started combing her hair back.

'That was good,' I told her, though truth to tell, I wanted more.

She ran her hands through her short back and sides, and checked the mirror. I noticed the heavy gold ring on the third finger of her right hand.

'I want more,' I said, and she looked alarmed. 'Oh. You're meeting someone.'

'I'm, you know, involved,' she mumbled.

'Don't worry,' I said. 'I don't want to marry you, Jools.'

I started dressing, deliberately bending and, sure enough, there came those hands again. This time, she pinned my face to the wall and fucked me from behind. I could see my eyes in the mirror and her sweating face as she made it fast. I wondered who she was meeting, and smiled as my whole body seized ecstasy.

'OK?' she asked.

'OK,' I said, and put my clothes on.

'I don't do this sort of thing,' she said.

'It suits you,' I said, 'and neither do I.'

One of us was lying, and as we left the loo, Jools seemed nervous. She paused and I took my bag and walked towards the taxi rank. I could hear someone shouting and furious and, as I glanced backwards, Jools stood like a naughty schoolboy beside a dumpy little woman with a pile of cases. She was pointing at me and Jools was shrugging, and I guess that was sweet domestic bliss.

Two

Niall had found himself a curved ceilinged flat in Islington – he called it *small but perfectly formed*, with its balcony high above the exhaust fumes and grime of the city. Room enough on the balcony for something pink that looked like a palm tree, two chairs and a table big enough for two glasses and a cocktail shaker.

'Darling,' he said, once the lift had spat me out at his door, 'what a healthy country glow you have – or is that the brandy? Let me feed you before we go on to the patio. Honestly, I feel like Rapunzel up here, sweetie. I'm thinking of buying a fucking wig to hang permanently from the balcony. But they've turned the old bingo hall into a club, darling, the Inferno, only streets away and it's seething with talent. Interested?'

'Not tonight, Josephine,' I said. 'I think I'll save all that for tomorrow.'

'Mm,' he said, 'so much better to see it in daylight, one can have such dreadful shocks otherwise. Or indeed give them.'

I laughed, remembering a whispered 6 am phonecall from Niall begging me to come round and be his sister, his mother, his girlfriend, his probation officer, anyone, in fact, to save him from the bit of trade he'd found lying beside him in the sweet grey dawn. I was also waiting for him to start one of his persistent interrogations about the state of my heart, but he didn't. We spent the evening on the balcony and he waxed lyrical about sex and sex, and urged me to put it about a bit. I told him about Jools and he laughed and hoped she would be at Pride the next day, complete with wife. Just for the hell of it.

'After all, darling,' he said, as we went to bed, 'use it or lose it, that's what I say.'

Morning found us fragile and our annual resolve to walk the length of the Pride March crumbled as it did every year. Niall made a thermos of cocktails and we preened ourselves into satin and silk and Lurex and denim and told each other how wonderful we looked. We always dressed from the skin outwards for Pride and nightclubs – as Niall said, there was no point in luring a little lust home to the horrors of grey Y-fronts or sensible knickers. I had bought black silk for my skin, a wisp of a thong and a bra that was almost invisible.

We took a taxi to the Park, and listened, as we did every year, to the cab driver moaning about streets being closed for a bunch of perverts. Niall slid out a bottle of nail varnish and graffiti-ed *we're here because we're queer* on the back of the driver's seat.

We hit the Park and made our camp beside the junction of four paths so all the gay world would see and be seen by both of us. Three drag queens on stilts strode by, screeching, a clown-faced unicyclist wearing only balloons whirled past, an army of leather men strolled across the grass, sipping tea. This year, the gay colour was the rainbow, and parrot wigs and painted chests gleamed in the sunshine. Everywhere, the smell of dope, the beat of music from the marquees, whistles and drums, fancy dress, flirting and posing. We drank cocktails and watched the open-air pantomime.

'Are you and Emilia the Groke still an item?' Niall said, 'or are you tarting?'

'Yes and yes,' I said, an easy mood filling me, fuelled by the first shot in a battlefield of Singapore Slings. I stretched on the soft municipal grass and felt the silky black thong caress me in all the right places as I breathed it in, gay life forms and balloons in pink and rainbow as far as the eye could see.

'Trollop!' said Niall. 'True love and one-nighters, darling? Mind, since she seems more absent than present, I can only approve.'

'I don't do True Love,' I told him.

And were the Groke – Goddess – and I *still an item*?

As You Desire Me

The dictionary defines *item* as follows.

1) A single article listed on a bill. *Well, she cost me plenty.*

2) A unit included in a collection or series. *Hmm.*

3) A separate matter for consideration. *Yeah, we were separate, and my god, did I ever give anything more consideration!*

4) A member of a set of minimal units. *That fitted well with being last on her list as I so often seemed to be.*

5) A bit of information, a detail. *Like, a minor detail?*

6) Also, likewise. *Well, it was becoming rather same-ish.*

'Trollop yourself,' I told Niall, 'you are sprawled there, all louche and lustful, exuding Paloma Picasso from every pore; your eyes have been out on stalks since we got here, and my god, I've even seen you drooling. Trollop I may be but, yes, Emilia and I are still an item.'

'Might I ask then,' Niall said, 'why she is not at your side for this annual queer bunfight?'

'She's working,' I said.

'Mm,' he said.

As the drunken afternoon wore on to the drunken evening, we lurched to the drag tent and laughed ourselves semi-sober, then hit the Inferno for a serious prowl.

15

Three

We settled in a corner where we could see all the coming and going, and soon Niall was making eyes at something lanky and fashionably unshaven in tan leather. I took a discreet bar-break until the lanky etc was sitting at our table, and let my eyes wander through the crowd.

I found myself looking at a group of vaguely familiar faces – Jesus! That could never be Zee! She hadn't seen me, so I studied her just to be sure. She was grinning like a wolf – one of her trademarks – but much thicker-set than when I knew her. She sauntered towards the bar and the walk was the same, a sort of punch-drunk cowboy strut. Amazing that half of London – including me – would have killed to be in her bed in those far-off basement days. She was still drinking pints and now it showed in the flesh around her once-taut waist, and the solid dip of flesh between her chin and neck.

Niall fluttered his hand to me and I joined him.

'This is Alberto,' he said. 'Alberto, this is my friend Alex. Alberto is Moroccan and trying to improve his English although *I* find his accent quite divine.'

'Hello,' said Alberto. 'It's a nice man?'

'It is,' I said.

'What are you staring at, darling?' Niall said.

'See her – all in black?'

'Lots of teeth?'

'Yes,' I said, 'that's Zee.'

'Never!' Niall said, 'Zee, the all-weather fuck-bunny? Well, it just shows that Baby Jesus must have been looking after you all those years ago, my love. What a lucky escape.'

I smiled.

'I think Alberto wants to dance, angel,' Niall murmured. 'Will you be all right?'

'Yes,' I said, 'I'm having fun.'

I watched Zee and her entourage swilling pints and let my mind wander back.

I was squatting in the East End with Zee, then the most beautiful woman in the world. My world. Well, I lived in the damp windowless basement and she lived everywhere else. And sometimes late at night we'd wind up in bed together if neither of us had anyone else that night. And Zee was in love with Mrs Jones who was *her* most beautiful woman in the world and Mrs Jones was living with Mr Jones, her husband.

And I thought I was in love with Zee; she was the queen of my heart and soul.

Apart from living in the basement, I was living in Hope.

Hope that Zee would one day look at me the way she looked at Mrs Jones, the way she looked when she was talking about Mrs Jones, or thinking about Mrs Jones. Sort of smouldering, starry-eyed and volcanic. Just the way I felt about Zee.

You should have seen her in those days!

She was a legend!

Zee was tall and lean, a sex machine who played pool while all the girls swooned and sweated over her taut, faded jeans, and the lean thighs and androgynous ass inside them. Zee bleached her hair with Ajax and cut it with a bread knife. She swore and drank like a navvy, snarling her upper-class, cut-glass inherited vowels to extinction. She fought like a kamikaze pilot on acid, smashing pool cues and tables and chairs and teeth.

Everyone on the scene was in love or lust with her, or they'd had her and hated her, or wanted her and loved her, or they'd had her and were friends, or she'd had their girlfriends, ditto and on and on.

I fell in love with her when she was blowing a saxophone in one of those god-awful punk funk bands that were all the rage at the time. Wrong. I fell in love with her when she was selling tickets at the door. Love at first sight, jaw bouncing on the floor, cunt on fire, no one wore underwear, bras had been ritually burned decades before, and knickers were a bourgeois affectation. The dress code of the dirty, dirty bitches! One look at Zee and I was tongue-tied, swallowing lakes of gin and tonic against the moment I'd get the nerve to tell her and more gin and tonic to have the nerve to tell her this was the real thing – it must be, it was just the way it happened on celluloid, just the way the songs told it.

And then the gig started and she was standing there with a saxophone. And fuck knows if she played it sweet or lousy, it was enough that she was standing there and I was seeing her, standing in the same room, on the same planet as her, only a few tables and chairs between us. No one has the right to be that good-looking but she was, and she knew it. There were pre-orgasmic groans every time she put her lips to the mouthpiece, and gasps of naked lust when she turned around and bent down to get some fucking thing out of her case, who gave a shit what. Her ass shone in bleached denim so tight it seemed painted on; she had a fuck-you rockstar's parrot plume of bleached hair, cheekbones to fight a duel over and the sort of mouth you could sit on for the rest of your life and never get tired.

Call it love, lust, use any fucking word you want; I was in it way over my head, swimming back to my chair like I was greased head to foot for a cross-channel marathon, clutching my glass by way of balance, thighs aflame, nipples tingling like they'd been clamped to a high-voltage battery.

I mean the band was crap – Lips 'n' Molasses, I think, was the name. Sounds sexy and sweet, which is why I'd gone, that's bullshit; it was them being a dyke band and me being a newly discovered dyke and always the chance of meeting Ms Right, or settling for Ms Will Do For Now. So it was the usual low-budget fuck-faced hall, somewhere purpose-built for jumble sales and Girl Guide Meetings and flood refugees to sleep in. Only tonight it was ours, with hand-done politically correct posters all over, *Reclaim The Night, Wimmin Against This and That,* and no toilet paper in the broken loos.

Lips 'n' Molasses was made up of a bass guitar – *chunka chunka hip thrust fucka!* – a violin – *tweedlee twiddly hee-haw di wee-wee* – a drum kit – *blit bla blam, shwishy wishy washy shittta* – two acoustic guitars – *mwah mwah nyah wah hah nying nying nyinga,* and then this seven-foot, vibrating G-spot blonde, pumping smoky sex 'n' sin through her loose, easy limbs and into every throbbing cell of my body. Every note bluesed and schmoozed – *feel me, finger me, fuck me, suck me dry...*

The beer was oil and soap and piss, the spirits were multi-coloured bubbles of paint stripper, the glasses were plastic and I had found Nirvana because of this fuck-bunny, dream-fingered woman playing saxophone – or murdering it, who cared, not me – gin-flavoured anti-freeze boiling through my veins from the geyser steaming between my legs.

Fucka wee wee mwah shitta nyinga – we are the forgohohotten ones! – *feel me, take, make me scream* – we are the wi-hi-himmin that time has given up on – *shwishy fucka blam blit nyinga shitta nyinga nyinga nyinga fuck...*

Lips 'n' Molasses took a break and I watched the saxophone player's lips turn the plastic glass into a crystal goblet, the puke-yellow lager into ambrosia. I lurched to the downstairs bar to mainline more 40% proof nail-varnish remover and bumped heavily and accidentally into this tough-looking woman who, thank Christ, just laughed and said: 'Lips 'n' fucking Molasses, more like shit and cyanide, eh?'

'Crap,' I howled, 'what you drinking?'

'All right,' she said, 'I'll get a table and double what you're having, you look fine on it.'

How come I was scoring with this one, when the lagoon of lust between my thighs was hot and flowing for the sax-sucker from heaven? But you never say no; well, I didn't, a flirt a day keeps the blues away and it beats the shit out of wallflower time and pretending you're cool.

Dream-fuck with the brassy sax was out of my league and the tough little number waving me over to the table looked like fun, so I went to her.

'Ta,' she said, 'I'm Alex.'

'Well, so am I,' I said, and we laughed into our drinks.

'Straight up?' she asked.

'Only way to fly,' I said.

Not seen you here before, fucking women, *does your head in,* non-monogamy does your head in, *fuck the next Lips 'n Molasses set,* three rounds later me and Alex were getting on just fine. There was no sex vibe but it didn't matter. We fit with each other, so I told her about the sax player.

'Mean and lean and blonde?' she said, curling her lip, 'Had her sort. Beautiful people are bastards. They never treat you right. Fuck! They don't have to; they can shit on your face and you'd thank them for the beauty pack. Just go and fucking tell her.'

Me?

'What's the worst thing that could happen?' said this other Alex.

'I dunno,' I said.

'You tell her you fancy her,' Alex said, 'and she tells you to fuck off. And then you're in exactly the same place as you are right now, getting smashed with me. And we're having a good time, aren't we?'

'Yeah,' I said, 'I'll just go and fucking tell her. Just don't go away.'

The other Alex unwound a leather strip from her wrist and pushed it into my hand.

'That's my soul you've got there,' she said. 'If I don't have that on my wrist every midnight, I shrivel up like a fucking balloon! Wheeeeeee! All the way round the room and straight down on the floor to get swept up with the dog-ends. Where the fuck would I go, anyway? I like meeting loonies. I'll get the drinks in. Now go on, girl, go for it!'

I tied the leather round my wrist and moon-walked to the stairs.

You know how your whole life just sometimes flashes in front of you? Time doesn't stand still; it ceases to exist and you're floating like an astronaut with this ridiculous movie playing out every ridiculous scene.

Well, that's what happened on this staircase, walking so slow you'd think I wore lead-soled boots, holding my place against a torrent of booze-starved women doing the lemming boogie to the bar.

It's two in the morning and I am alone in a strange bed. Next door, a woman coughs and I sit up, wondering. I take her next cough as a signal and take my life in hands and go next door, not realising that I am about to give my heart and my life away.

Just like that.

I open her bedroom door and she is lying there in the moonlight. I sit on the side of her bed – what's the matter, she says, can't you sleep? I see me, anxious teenager, don't belong anywhere that'll have me, clutching the Oxfam silk of my dressing gown like a lifebelt. I'm going down in bubbles and my lungs are full...

This is the moment that changes my whole life.

Suddenly I was at the top of the stairs, the lemmings had all come out of the Lips 'n' Molasses gig, the doorway to the hall was a cliff edge and the sax player was packing up right at the other end. All the lights were on and I was here to see her. To tell her. Tell her what?

I wrapped my fingers round Alex's leather soul, and crossing the bare floor was like climbing a glass mountain. Or crossing Antarctica. I knew as I dragged my heart like a dog-sledge across the endless waste of wooden boards that I was coming to another moment that could change my life, and if I said what I wanted to say and she said *fuck off* or anything like then my habit of worshipping from afar would blow her right out of the dream gallery.

The dream gallery was all mine.

Every woman who'd ever brought a sparkle to my eye or a flush to all four cheeks, each lovely face and form that floated my boat and got my mojo working, the soaking gusset girls, as Niall christened them. Starting with the woman in the moonlit bedroom – before I knew her better. Cher, the woman in the bakers in Hammersmith, Anne Bancroft, the paper-shop lady in Edinburgh, Shirley McClaine, a motorbike lady cop in California, Martina Navratilova, an Irish nurse sedating Zee in the Mile End casualty, Katharine Ross, a red-sequinned stripper in Southampton, Christine Lahti…

Food for fantasy and never a cross word.

Until the other Alex had jeered me up these stairs, the sax strutter was all lined up to join the dream gallery. I had glued my whole being to hers, absorbed the wonder of her into me so I could replay her at will. I hesitated, only feet from her unbelievably gorgeous back, picturing myself safe and un-lovelorn back at the bar.

But it was too late: she turned round and looked at me.

Her eyes were smoky grey like sea you want to dive into at dawn, grey blue like the sky before sunrise, the rays of the new day turning speckles of cloud to gold, blue like a wood hazed through with bluebells. And looking straight at me.

Her cheekbones – well, to hell with the anatomy lesson, I was just fired to reach out my incandescent fingertips to her skin, learn her by touch.

'What?' she said and orchestras played around that smoky syllable.

'Brilliant,' I said, 'I just wanted to say…'

…*that I love you.*

'We're not that good,' she said, although she was pleased.

'No,' I said. *Just fuckin' tell her!* 'Yes. I mean, I think you're amazing.'

She liked that a lot and managed to look flattered and amused. Then she raised an eyebrow, waiting for what would come out of my stupid mouth next.

'I mean,' I said, 'I just, well I know it's corny and all that, just you're amazing, just – oh shit, I don't know.'

'I've always suffered from having a pretty face,' she said.

'It's not just that,' I said wildly, thinking how do I tell her about the stardust at her feet and fingertips, how do I tell her about the halo shining brighter than a Pre-Raphaelite Madonna, how do I tell her?

'I'd really like to see you some more,' I said, waiting for *fuck off* or laughter.

'Well,' she said, 'I'll give you my address. We're touring till the end of June. Come up and see me after that.'

She scrawled across a piece of paper and handed it to me.

'I'm Zee,' she said. 'Be in touch.'

'I'm Alex,' I said and stumbled away, suddenly aware of the rest of the band packing up and there was a giggle as I crossed the hall; no doubt Zee had groupies flocking everywhere they went – she had been so cool about the volcano of feeling I'd lifted the lid on.

To hell with that!

I floated down the stairs, back to the bar and glided to the side of the other Alex. I closed my eyes against her cheeky, brown-eyed curiosity, gulped the drink she'd got me and grinned like Liberace's piano.

Four

It was coming on for Christmas when I saw Zee again.

In the London A – Z, she lived only a square and a half from the docks, and I took one big red bus after another, buildings growing taller and sootier as I rode. Me with a bottle of wine, flowers, a small but real Christmas tree, and people with bulging shopping bags and red noses, and the slatted floor all dirt and slush.

At the end of Zee's street was a monolithic tower block, and her house was in a terrace like *Coronation Street* when it first came out. They'd filled the monolith from that street and a dozen others, and then the drop-outs and dykes had squatted the newly decreed sub-standard housing with its open fires and outside plumbing, rent-free and PC. After them, the yuppies would move in, buying houses in pairs and knocking them through. And the original people would look over their concrete balconies and despise the squatters, then envy the yuppies and know that somehow, somewhere, as usual, they'd been ripped off.

And academics would analyse the phenomenon of squatting and talk about the communist cell as a model of subversion. Bullshit. Squatting was cheap and the only rules were what you made up yourself. It suited someone like Zee whose income was sporadic, whose lifestyle was armchair anarchy glamorised by her predatory sexual habits and reputation.

There was paint on some of the doors on the street, but not the one bearing the weather-stained shadow of Zee's house number.

I knocked.

Zee opened the door, stark naked and fabulous in the chill December air. She pressed her beautiful lips to mine and led me to her snow-white bed, ripped my clothes from me and we were a tangle of flesh on flesh.

I knocked again.

A pigeon with mutilated toes shat on the doorstep beside me. Some people say that means good luck – or is that when they shit on your head? When Zee answered the door she was wearing only a silk kimono and her smile was a magic carpet that flew me to Paradise.

I don't have a clue what Zee was wearing when she finally answered the door. I do know she was knicker-dropping gorgeous, better even than I remembered and her grey-blue eyes made everything else disappear. She gave me this soft, goofy smile, and said come in and I did, and followed her along bare floorboards and scarred paint tacked over with posters, past a chewed banister and downstairs to under the street where her basement kitchen and she were steaming and exotic. I do know that looking at her ass while I was walking behind her sent a knife blade of liquid desire through me; her shoulders were broader and I was wetter, her hair was wilder and I was soaking and altogether more frenzied than I had thought possible.

My head rang with a pulsing heat, and I knew that I had just walked into a life that was a compass direction further than anything I'd ever been able to dream of. Or ultimately have nightmares about.

Her kitchen was that middle-class mucky clutter of jars of spices and herbs, an ingrained cigarette-burned wooden table, assorted chairs. A cat lay asleep by a fruit bowl containing three gangrened bananas and a bitter and twisted pear. A huge saucepan steamed on the stove. This siren cooked? Postcards and notes pinned everywhere, plastic kiddy toys, a forest of empty wine bottles as dusty as the finest cellar could boast. Sequins trailed from the scorched lampshade. There was a sepia patina everywhere, which looked Dickensian and romantic, although it probably came from the seventy or so unfiltered Park Drive Zee consumed daily.

In those days, smoking was still an attractive feature. Bite the smoke and you're angry; slowly exhale and you're randy; offer a cigarette and your entire body and all its erotic possibilities are a free gift, taped to the packet.

I like the sort of voice smoking gives you if you're truly dedicated.

'I'll put the kettle on,' Zee said, blowing smoke, her shoulders swaggering to the cracked sink.

I was still standing there with my Christmas tree and everything.

'For you,' I said, sliding bags to the floor.

'For me?' she said. 'Everything?'

'The whole lot,' I said, including myself. I tried to make it a Barry White drawl, but it came out more Olive Oyl.

Her eyes gleamed wickedly as she moved round the cluttered confines of the room like a panther. Somehow, she could slink in three short steps, and the cracked lino shimmered by her feet and assumed the elegant patina of marble. The green and grey enamel of the old stove was blessed by her touch, and spat a magic ring of flames in violet amber and turquoise, and the water in the blackened kettle hissed on the metal as it touched the flames.

Beside the sink was the only window in the room. City grey, it filtered the weak winter light, but beyond the glass on the subterranean wetness of blackened stone grew a huge sap-green fern and a cluster of dandelion leaves and, for me, it was the hanging gardens of Babylon, framing the fabulous outline of Zee's face. She stirred the saucepan with a pair of wooden salad tongs and turned to me with a wolfish grin, raising the dripping tongs to show me something blue-and-white striped and steaming.

'Boiled knickers,' she said. 'A great lesbian delicacy.'

Where I came from long ago you didn't talk about knickers. In Zee's basement, I didn't even wear them – why bother once the bra's been burned, even if takes half a can of lighter fluid to reduce the elastic to ash – and smoke gets in your eyes.

I remembered the bra-burning party at the women's centre, and how everyone was snogging and groping and I wound up in the wrecked garden getting fucked stupid under a cloudy moon. And then I'd gone home with me and wondered if I'd ever find Ms Right or if she'd been run over by a bus or emigrated.

I thought of all this while Zee poured tea and I imagined her naked and crossed every nerve end and vein in my body and hoped she'd be The One. She just sat opposite me, smoking, her slate-grey eyes creeping into my soul like mistletoe into the sap of an oak.

Of course, her name wasn't Zee and she wasn't Ms Right.

She had worn out her welcome in most of the bent bedrooms and bars of London by the time I sat drinking tea with her. Few could take the whole deal that was Zee. Smouldering, sexy, androgynous – yes *please!*

But Zee liked to drink until her mouth spat venom over a coiling gut full of vodka. Then her fists flew and she smashed doors and heads and glasses and relationships, and I knew none of this when I moved into the basement room next to the kitchen.

But she had a way of making you feel you were the only person in the room; she exuded the confidence that beautiful people take so much for granted it's electric, magnetic. Sirens, sex-goddesses, the ones who've always got so much adoration they expect it – hell, they look the part and most of us are happy to give it to them. They get the leading role, our hearts, our thoughts, flowers, sweet music, all our waking hours and our dreamtime too.

Including overdrafts and tears and late-night phone calls and all of this we forget in the first flush, blinded, bound and confounded by beauty.

And Zee was beautiful in those days, by anyone's terms.

Beautiful people don't have to learn good manners or even work on a personality, since their looks guarantee them a captive audience, just like the other Alex had said.

We ordinary types work like hell to make ourselves attractive – we can make people laugh and we know where to take people for drinks and dinner and days out – and god, are we ever good in bed!

I looked across the nightclub to where the older Zee stood with her nth pint.

The last time I'd seen her, she had been brought home in a taxi, and it took three of us to get her to bed as she thrashed around, punching the air and cursing. Snarling like a wolf, she had sunk her teeth into my skull and drawn blood before she passed out. She came roaring into my room at four that morning and fucked me so intensely that for a moment I had wondered if she really meant it. Only then she'd beaten the living shit out of me and crashed back upstairs.

I sipped my drink and felt the terror of that dark attack, how bruised and utterly alone I'd been on the floor once she'd gone. Then the icy, gritty chill of the empty streets before sunrise when I'd walked and walked and walked, trying to work out what the hell I was going to do next. I'd burned a dozen bridges to move into Zee's then-charmed circles.

Niall and Alberto dropped into the chairs beside me.

'Seen anything?' Niall asked me.

'Just a ghost or two,' I said.

'I think it's bed-time,' Niall said. 'Alberto is on early shift; what a shame he can't stay. Let's taxi, darling.'

As we left the club, Zee was begging some impassive, crew-cut girl to come home with her. It looked like she was getting nowhere, and I laughed out loud.

Five

I rang Porridge the next day to meet her for a coffee. Her voice was warm and friendly until she knew it was me, then each word slashed a venomous contempt. Ouch.

'Really, dear,' Niall said, 'are you surprised? She's had more than a year of your absence to find out just what a tart you were during the death-throes of your relationship. Dykes gossip so! I've seen her around on the scene, dear, putting it about. You knew she'd hear the whole grisly lot! And *you* ended it, ergo, you are the Wicked Lady. Speaking of which, would you like one, and we'll call it brunch? I even have a croissant or two, darling, seeing as how I am an Islington queen these days.'

So we dipped and sipped and let the watery sun wash away our hangovers.

'Just say fuck it,' he said. 'If Emilia the Groke is making you unhappy, fuck her too! I know you want to, but really! She may have the surface panache of Brunhilde, but her soul – such as it has been described to me – would appear to belong more to melodrama than grand opera. Wagner is dreary anyway, after one is nineteen. Find yourself a bit of Mozart, dear, a bit of class. I have hopes for you and Miss X – now *she* brightens you up no end.'

I promised to do my best.

On the way to the station, I went into a florist's shop and ordered two bouquets. One for Emilia, of course, with hopes for a blossoming future. And one for Miss X, for the times she made it all bearable. I felt cheeky and wicked as I scrawled the two cards. Maybe I should send one to the cute-assed peroxide number I half had my eye on? No – we would be meeting for dinner that evening. I'd deliver her flowers in person.

Niall had given me a pink thermos of Wicked Lady for the train. *Stick to brandy, dear, it cheers you so!* And it did. Time slipped by, green and not-so-merry old England through grey-smeared glass and a shadow reflection of me, hangover-pale. York flashed by without a pang and by the time I was home I was hair-of-the-dog rosy and ready for fun.

I taxi-ed back via an off-licence and a florist, then there was time to tart myself up to the eyeballs so that the cute-assed, peroxide number would feel instantly as randy as I did thinking of her. Hell, we might even skip dinner and just go to bed with one of the champagne bottles. Although she'd said she was cooking and I knew she liked to do this and be appreciated.

I lay in the bath and thought of Emilia.

Fuck it!

I mainlined a neat Metaxa Seven Star and brushed my teeth. Be here now. Or if that doesn't suit, then busk it. I dressed in silk and denim and a perfume made from bergamot and limes, smoothed on a cream that promised I'd never get any lines, and ordered a cab and told my reflection that a cute ass and peroxide bob as flaunted by Chris would do me fine for now. She could do me any way she wanted, and I would certainly do her whatever way she wanted me to. That was a nice thought. I sprawled in the cab, anticipating.

A stranger met me at the door.

The living/dining room was full of women and the cute peroxide ass was messing around in the kitchen. I must have betrayed a little of the surprise I felt, though I tried to turn it to cool, because one of the women smirked a little.

'We invited ourselves, Alex! Chris said you'd arrive bearing champagne...'

Talk of the town, huh, or gossip of the self-important part of town Chris hung out with. Miss X would never have pulled a trick like this – Miss X being a benchmark for a lovely and casual *affaire*. I put one bottle of champagne on the table and watched the icy dew run down the surface like sweat or tears.

'I wouldn't want to disappoint you,' I drawled, strolling up to my cute-assed floozie, air-kissing her cheek, giving her flowers, giving her a look intended to express total lust and amusement. She had the grace to blush ever so slightly and I would not look away.

'How was Pride?' she asked, shaking snow-peas in sesame oil in a wok.

'Fucking fantabulosa, dear,' I said. 'You must introduce me to all the girls.'

I was angry – surprises do not please me. Well, this one, anyway. It meant deferring the lust that had seemed so certain when we arranged this evening. It also meant having to act some more – I had anticipated an audience of one, after all. But now we were seven, I'd just have to make the best of it. I noticed Chris's wall display of Le Creuset everything, her limited-edition prints, the original pottery artefacts scattered here and there, and felt that I wouldn't mind being another trophy in her collection.

I went to the loo to decide on my role. Her loo was good too, a mural of stiff-nippled nudes languishing in a rain of gold, a real sponge twice the size of Einstein's brain, a bath big enough for two if you were feeling friendly, an Ali Baba washing basket, draped with skimpy, coffee-coloured lace and satin. Bath Oil called Sensuous and Erotic and Orgasm. OK.

I glanced into her bedroom as I went back downstairs. A big wide bed in black wood with four half-posts carved and spiked like flames, more pictures of pre- and post-orgasmic nudes, a clutter of jewellery. And lots of mirrors. What a pleasant playroom. I sauntered back to the girls – and Chris – to start the game.

I'd decided to be a bohemian intellectual sex-goddess and flirt with the assembled company. Chris was one of those women who gets turned on by jealousy. You don't get into the knickers of a well-travelled lush by wishing and hoping. You play games and manipulate: for someone like Chris, a dinner party is foreplay, and yes, I was playing for her, but damned if I'd make it either too easy or too obvious.

After a while, I felt like we were understudying for roles in *Snow White*, the seven of us. Sleepy went home around ten, Dopey mumbled through a series of joints. Grumpy tried to set the cock-eyed world to rights. Sneezy's allergies – no one ever admits to anything as common as a cold – forced her home at 10.30. One of us was even a real Doc and I used a big-style eye flirt on her, body language pure Esperanto. I was pleased to notice Chris noticing this and sliding in a few *I know her better* remarks to undercut the Doc. And Chris herself? She was playing Bashful and asked me to be DJ as an excuse for flinging me compliments about my good taste. Well, didn't that make me Happy, so I DJ-ed Charlie Parker, knowing jazz would make her drink more, feeling herself in a smoky cafe in Paris in the disaffected 40s or 60s. And the more she drank, the more I could drink and then our tongues could loosen up any way they damn well pleased. I lined up Edith Piaf to add to the effect then pure schmaltzy sex-sleaze courtesy of Nina Simone, Marvin Gaye and Bob Marley.

Edith Piaf was when Doc and Grumpy and Dopey left us alone, the way we should have been in the first place. I concentrated on their shoes: DMs, sandals and hiking boots – imaging them hit the floor and make for the night air. It always works.

By then, it was around midnight and Chris demonstrated her body-hug at the front door. I changed the music to hip-grinding reggae and sprawled with my feet on a chair. A cheroot and a sloosh of wine were my props.

'They do talk!' said the cute peroxide ass, flinging herself onto the sofa, seeking shreds of small talk in the scene I'd set.

'They're nice,' I lied, 'and this seems to be the last of the wine.'

'Oh dear,' she said, scrambling to her feet, 'that sounds like disaster. I must be in the wrong house.'

She crashed around in the kitchen and came back through, giggling, with an armful of bottles.

'There's Blue Curaçao, Tia Maria, vodka, Strega, some foul thing with a dead newt in it, and some Greek brandy,' she said.

'Sounds like instant diabetes,' I said, 'apart from the brandy and the newt juice.'

'Bugger you,' she said, 'I've been trying to get the other horrible lot drunk for ages. Let me find some suitable glasses for the destruction of the last of my Greek brandy. I thought you might go for the newt.'

I looked at the white and grey pickled eyes distorted in the curved bottle.

'You should display that,' I said. 'No, make mine a large Greek. And do have one yourself.'

'Bloody cheek,' she said.

She was stumbling as she went back to the kitchen, so I decided to change the music. I didn't want a weep-on-my-shoulder early morning, unless it was post-orgasmic tears of ecstasy. Santana should do it, I thought – it usually hit the spot for stoned-out, post-hippy survivors like Chris.

And it did.

Five gulps into resin-tanged fire, and she was off with memories of a Mediterranean holiday on an unspoilt island, lots of sun and lots of sex and very few clothes. She was a woman who refused to be older, this cute peroxide ass, hovering somewhere way past where life begins. She could have passed for early thirties in the right light, and she knew it and liked it that way. Grey would never be allowed to stray into her hair, and fat would never be allowed to squat in any cell of her body. She had been around and around, many times around the blocks and icebergs of marriage and sex and romance, and I liked that.

I could never cope with having any kind of thing beyond one night with someone younger than me. Imagine not being able to say Woodstock or Joan Armatrading or Joan Baez without giving footnotes. I laughed at the ridiculous train of thoughts riding on a tank full of booze around the lazy, rose-tinted yesteryears, when being a poser was an ambition, not a rather embarrassing memory.

We talked and drank and listened to the songs that meant that somewhere we would always be young. Nude beaches, pop festivals, protest marches, maxi skirts, headbands, beads, bells and flowers. Dope. The spectacular drunks and outrageous combinations of alcohol. We shrieked with laughter at the daft behaviour we'd thrown ourselves into.

By the time I slid Edith Piaf back onto the turntable, we had no regrets, me and Chris; we'd made our confessions, absolved each other and groaned through our penances. Our souls were Persil-clean, the very fabric of our beings conditioned and smooth again.

Timing was of the essence now, and that was a huge challenge since I had just started seeing double. I went to the loo and drank gallons of water from the tap, caressing the flimsy café au lait underwear on the basket by the sink, not giving a damn if it was yes or no with Chris, just reckless and knowing whatever happened we could blame it on the moonshine. Blame it on the boogie.

Downstairs again, she'd made coffee.

'Getting a bit foggy,' she said. 'Don't worry, I haven't gone sober on you.'

I sat back on my chair and swung my les up again.

'Chris,' I said, 'do you want to go to bed with me?'

'Yes, I do,' she said straight away, 'of course I do, damn you – are you always this direct?'

'I think I'm pretty fucking subtle,' I told her, willing her to look in my eyes.

She got up and came to stand beside me. I put my arm round

her waist and sucked her nipple through the silk of her blouse, my other hand stroking the sweet curves of her ass. She leaned into me, her mouth brushing my neck. I held her close and tight and slid my hand under her skirt, caressing her thighs, massaging the soft skin of her flat belly. The heel of my hand registered silk and lace and hair and heat. I pushed my had into the firm V of wiry hair and my hand parted the wetness there. She thrust against me and swallowed my fingers; my thumb played against the heat of her, pinned there by taut satin. She dug her hands into my shoulders and hung her head into my spine.

'Let's go to bed,' she gasped.

'Later,' I said and half-carried her to the sofa where she'd been teasing me ever since we'd been alone.

The urge to simply fuck her beat through my head, pin down her hands and fuck her senseless. Have her scream *yes* and mean it, have her scream *no* and not mean it, have her talk filthy the way I knew she would, and beg me to go on, and beg me to stop with her words while her body demanded more...

So I stripped her, poured a little brandy into her navel, sucked it off and fed it into her open mouth. She shuddered against me, tried to pull me on top of her, clawed at my jacket, grabbed my belt and called me *bastard* when I wouldn't give in.

I stood and stripped for her, watching her hand flutter over her naked breasts. I sipped more brandy and came down over her very slowly, watching her face like a hawk, how her eyelids fluttered and her tongue ran along her lips. Her thighs spread-eagled and I stroked her there so gently it was driving her mad. My thigh snuggled between hers and I held her slender waist, held her tight until her ass was heaving against me like the tide beating at the confines of a sea wall.

And now I was ready too.

My thigh was sliding on the juice flowing from deep within her. The electric skin on my hand met a monsoon powering through her, and an earthquake of proud and tender flesh lunged against me. Her thigh drove against my cunt and, truth to tell, I could have come in five seconds flat. But I held back – I wanted to play big girls' games. I took hold of one of her wrists and pinned it deep into the cushion by her head. Her other arm flew up and it was like starting down a runway in a great big plane. The roaring rose through my body and I lunged into her, hard and slow. I like to be sure before I let fly – and remember, this is a lady I am dealing with, even if she's whispering filth between teeth-grinding gasps of desire, even if her breath whistles deep to her navel and every wild sound of her screams for more.

My hand was being tugged off my arm.

Somehow I worked my thumb free and worked it round the whorls of her sex. Her thigh clenched round my back and my ass worked against her other thigh and my ears were ready to explode – and it was take-off. I banged into her as crudely as a teenager, told her she was a bitch, a fucking, beautiful bitch and I was going to have her as many times as she could take it and more. She said *yes, yes, yes* and *yes* to all of this.

She was almost mile-high. My mouth sought hers and her tongue was mine and I sucked her face to the same rhythm as her cunt sucked my hand; our faces ate each other, and one of her hands flew free to grab my ass and force me faster and faster. I stopped and tore her hand from me. Her eyes and mine were wild with danger and domination.

Then I let her wrists free and she clung to me and I wasn't fucking her any more; we were together, rolling on to the floor like serpents entwined, her legs gripping my spine, and my captive hand became her as her climax started. She growled as my fingers spread fire on the lips of her sex and as I took her, I went with her.

She lay, jerking and muttering *bastard* over and over and I thrust in slow, slow motion, feeling waves fizz through every cell of my body, like falling out of a plane, feeling the same waves possess her until she lay like one dead. I crouched over her, like a lion over its prey, watching the pulse in her neck, the breath shifting the curves of her breasts. She didn't move.

I sat astride her and lit a cigarette and she looked up at me and smiled, her eyes glittering in the candlelight.

'Now we go to bed,' I said.

She took my hand and stumbled along beside me. I slid my thumb into the cleft of her cute ass as we walked.

'Got to pee,' she said.

So I lay on her bed feeling like a maharajah and watched her walk towards me.

'Put something on,' I said. 'I want to watch you take it off.'

'What sort of something?' she asked, like a child trying to please.

'Black lace,' I said, 'feed my fantasy.'

Which was to watch every move she made and she knew how to make them. She stretched into a see-through black basque and walked around a little, pretending like I wasn't there. Then she stood staring at me, and teased her body free, pale and naked in the half darkness.

I pulled her down beside me and her flesh felt fabulous.

'Fantasy,' she said, 'what other fantasies do you have, Alex?'

'You want me to tell you or show you?'

'Just do it,' she said.

I had this sudden powerful picture of fucking her cute ass, doggy-style, one hand on her neck, riding her ass like she was a half-broken colt.

So I did.

And then we collapsed together and crash-landed into deep sleep.

Six

Next day, I woke around eleven. There was a cold cup of tea next to the bed and strands of peroxide-white hair on the navy pillow case. My head had a demolition gang working inside it and my mouth was about as inviting as a navvy's spittoon. I reeked of sex and sweat, and the memories of fucking with Chris buzzed through my brain as I swam through crude brilliant daylight to the bathroom. I was grinning as I tumbled a handful of lilac crystals into the water. What a lady, what a night!

I raided her kitchen for coffee, orange juice, woman-size headache pills, vitamins, minerals, everything my body needed for resurrection. Gulping a foaming glass of seltzer into my aching liver, I lined up all these morning-after remedies by the bath and wondered about ringing the mistress of the house by way of good morning. Maybe later when my voice graduated from croak to growl. Christ knows how she'd got to work. I choked my way through my first cigarette and my head floated up, up and away. I scrubbed my teeth and lay back in the foam with the second, feeling my head settle comfortably back onto my neck.

It would have been nice to wake up with Chris and have her at the other end of this bath.

Maybe you've ruined a beautiful friendship.

Uh oh.

Where the hell had that come from? It was the fluting, sanctimonious voice of Sister Mary Misery, a residue of my good Catholic girl childhood with its statutory ball and chain of guilt. Catholicism is like herpes – it never goes away. Sister Mary always came to visit any time I have real bad girl fun, trying to clamp my guts in a chastity belt of cold and heavy fear.

Sexual intercourse is permitted only within the bonds of Holy Matrimony, for the purposes of procreation.

Well, the nuns saw the world and its ways in black and white just like the neo-burka habits they wore. But I was a teenager when the first inklings of Technicolor blazed into my world on the wings of desire, and nothing the sisters said made sense any more. Particularly since it was one of their number who had lit the fire with kisses and caresses stolen in a late-night cloister. Sister Angela with the face of an angel and full warm lips like a Michelangelo cherub. Any hymn we sang mentioning love, I would try to catch her eye.

To hell with Sister Angela, and Sister Mary Misery – hey, Kemo Sabe, who needs angst anyway? And what friendship? Chris and I hardly knew each other.

To hell with the nuns! Mae West said: *Too much of a good thing can be wonderful.* She also said: *There's no such thing as a good girl gone bad, just a bad girl found out.*

My main concern, once I'd jeered the nun's tales out of my head, was that last night had been our first, last and only – it's a real drag when you want a one-night stand to clone and evolve into more, and she doesn't. It's always the ones when you wake up and think, oh shit, who the hell are you, and the memory of what you were doing shines in their eyes – the ones that want to make coffee and talk and you're desperately trying to recall their name – they're the ones who inevitably want to stick around for more. You invent a butch and jealous long-term lover about to be released from Holloway, a nervous breakdown, a job abroad. And for a while, you get hangdog looks in your favourite drinking places and have to go elsewhere for a while or tough it out. Kind of tedious.

But I felt there would be more with Chris. It was pretty clear she liked to lie back and be done unto, and that was fine. She'd gone apeshit and fierce when I fucked her ass and told me that was one of her favourite fantasies too.

And there was also the matter of Emilia, the one I felt closest to falling in love with, the one I was wining and dining at 6.30 that evening. Sister Mary Misery tried to start an infidelity guilt trip with me, but I drowned her in strong coffee – how the hell can you be faithful to someone you hardly ever see? Years ago I'd been unquestioningly faithful to Jodie, and what had that brought but tears and a near breakdown? I'd tried fidelity with Porridge and though we saw each other most days, the cosy, middle-aged bed death freaked me off so much I swore I'd never ever make a promise I can't keep again. I loved Emilia when she was there. If she wanted anything else she could let me know about it.

I looked around Chris's bedroom and knew I'd be back there.

But now it was time to go.

I sometimes wondered if I felt I loved Emilia simply because she was elusive.

Maybe.

Which is why there was no resemblance between me at five o'clock that day and the me that had swanned in on Chris the night before, not giving a fuck.

Which made me infinitely more desirable. If you want it, but not too bad, you get it and when you really – heart and soul and aching cunt – desire someone, you get strung along, strung out and played like a fish on a hook. I knew that so I was acting cool. Well, I would when she got here, the Groke, the Goddess, Princess Emilia. Her life was a series of power games, I realised that much, although I liked to think of her as vulnerable and flawless.

Another bath, a mega-wallow with hot wax on my hair, pure silk everything pressed to perfection, wine in the fridge, clean sheets, Celestial Sky incense, a cologne that smelt of tangerines and musk. Emilia had really been a hippy – well, she'd run away with a rock band somewhere in her teens – OK, maybe just for a few weeks, but it was one of her best stories, and she liked perfumes with a *bouffe* of patchouli.

I lay naked on the sofa with a half glass of neat vodka and let my hand play around my cunt. I was good, but good. Well into reaching parts of me that few get to know about. Sometimes someone wants to know, but mostly they're into what does it for them. And that's fine. I rang Chris just before she was leaving work and got my voice used to talking again, securing a dinner date the following night. She worked for some worthy social development agency and had theatre tickets for tonight, and she would – she said – have asked me to go with her if what had happened the night before had happened before last night. I felt a near-orgasm fizz through my body and teased it back, drinking in her polite professional voice, a real contrast to the screaming banshee howling obscenities while I fucked her less than twenty-four hours before. Mists of colour sparkled in my head as ecstasy flooded me and I asked her favourite colour. She said purple, predictably, and asked why. I said I was just curious and let her play with that, we said *au revoir* and I felt a million times better for calling her. Like coming up for air before the deep-sea diving that happened with Emilia, sometimes amazing, but so often dark and terrifying, like getting the bends when you've stayed down for too long.

Emilia – I let my fingertips draw out the ebb tide of orgasm and tossed the last of the vodka down my throat.

She had promised to ring me as she was leaving, but I'd be mind blown if she actually did. We'd said 6.30, and I'd booked a table for 8.30. I kind of hoped, if she came when she said she would, that we'd get to screw each other stupid before we ate. Huh!

She was unlikely to be here before 7.30, so I mixed a vodka and lime and lay back down.

I was tingling with pleasure and this time I played myself real slow. Pure heaven. Which made me feel sentimental, so I rang Miss X at her office and embarrassed the hell out of her by describing exactly what I was planning to do with her the next time we met.

'Can I make a suggestion?' she said.

'You can try.'

'My place, day after tomorrow. I'll cook, then we can spend all our pennies on really good wine.'

'You're on,' I said.

5.30. Time to watch a movie.

And tomorrow night and the one after were taken care of, whatever trauma the Goddess/Groke happened to dump on me. I picked *Casablanca*, seeing I know it off by heart, and three vodka limes later, Sam was playing it again and I decided, fuck it – if she's not here by eight, I'm getting out of here and going on the pull. I might even swan into the theay-tah foyer and pick up the cute peroxide floozie after she'd done her arty-farty community duty. Or I could just hit the clubs instead and drag anything willing and trashy home to play with.

And are these the thoughts of a woman waiting for the one she loves?

Hey, I cried salt lakes through Porridge and any other damn woman I've used the L word with. These were my thoughts, and I was the woman doing her best to steel herself against having WELCOME tattoo-ed across her back. I was fighting being in Love with Emilia, and I planned to come out of this one with my heart and sanity more or less in one piece.

Vodka burned the word *eternal* across my tongue and a woman in the movie sang 'La Marseillaise'...

I surprised myself by thinking of Jodie and the times I'd prepared to meet her, sunny days by a waterfall, swimming in a river golden with dawn, slow kisses at sunset. And tears before bedtime. To hell with the miasma they call love and the shifting sands where you find yourself struggling against sinking. In Love, you are lost.

7.20.

I dressed, adding cufflinks shaped like dice. Emilia liked that sort of thing. I scrubbed my teeth and lit another cigarette, dithering about more vodka.

Bogart and Bergman did the right thing in black and white as the front door opened. Only Emilia and I have keys, and my heart thundered louder than the extravagant music over the credits. I lit a candle, slooshed out more vodka and made myself look absorbed in finding another video.

What fucking time do you call this and why didn't you call? I'm not your slave. I do have a life separate from you and maybe the whole of it should get that way! Fifty-fifty makes a good friendship but this is ninety-fucking-nine to one. I am a very desirable woman and I have the notches on my headboard to prove it. So wise up, bitch – give or go.

It's maybe a good thing the Goddess/Groke was low on ESP.

'Hello,' she said, in that breathy voice that sent my head spinning.

'Hi there,' I said without looking round.

'I got caught up,' she said.

'Uh?' I said.

'I'm late, she said, 'I'm always late, darling, I'm so sorry.'

'I hadn't noticed,' I said. 'What's the time, anyway?'

'Late,' she said. 'God, Alex, you look lovely.'

She bent over me and sunk her head into my neck.

'Just adorable,' she said.

'You're kinda cute yourself,' I said, turning my head to kiss her, drooping my eyelids so she couldn't read the bruised anger in my eyes.

Emilia was a hell of a kisser. Her lips were soft and full, and her tongue melted into all my oral G-spots. It blew me that she kissed like Sister Angela all those years ago, and I strained round to hold her and float in her wonderful arms. We wound up on the floor, thighs clamped around each other like limpets and I thought, to hell with dinner, but some canny little sixth sense told me no.

'You want to eat or get eaten?' I said to her earlobe, my face swathed in her long hair.

'Both,' she said, winding her hands round my shoulders, lying her head back in a way that was almost irresistible.

'Let's go, then,' I said, standing and lighting a cigarette.

My sixth sense was right; I could see it in her face. It surprised her – hell, she was used to me just about on my knees begging for it, and the surprise gave me an edge. It also gave me time to seduce her – if I charmed the waiters and commented on other women in the restaurant, she always got horny as hell to prove she was the only girl in the world. Which she was – when she was there. And for all the time that she was there.

I rang for a cab and she sat on my knee kissing me while we waited. I slipped the buttons of her blouse and held her breast in my hand, in my mouth, against my cheek.

'I feel very randy,' she breathed.

'Good,' I said, 'I'll deal with that later.'

'Promise?' she said.

'Betcha life, woman,' I said, 'I have designs on your body.'

'Lovely, she said, 'lovely.

Seven

She did various outrageous things with her elegantly curved thumb and the steamy crotch of my silk pants as we taxi-ed through the night.

I let her.

I was enjoying the attention; it made a change. Usually she spent rides like this telling me all the things that had gone wrong in the time we'd been apart. And how she had risen, phoenix-like, above them all. How she'd vanquished the endless rabble who seemed set on destroying her – the taxman, the bin men, the gas men, the butcher, the baker and Uncle Tom Cobleigh and all.

Her inner traumas – ex-husband, ex-lovers, Marcie – she generally saved 'till bedtime and she'd talk herself to sleep in my frustrated arms.

When she was there, I was all but In Love and I was going to be the one who understood her, the one to give her the freedom she longed for; I would heal her deepest scars and kiss all the nightmares goodbye.

If she wanted me that way.

That was some of what she had found lacking in everyone else, or so she said.

She said I was so good at listening. Funny, when I was with Miss X, or the cute peroxide ass, or any of the other sluts and sirens who shared my time or my bed, I found that conversation was a two-way process. But Emilia had come to loom larger than life – my life, anyway – I was addicted to her, ever since that hug – or was it the Sister Angela kiss – I wanted to know her inside out, to précis her life story from the series of myself-as-heroine cameos she'd told me:

Well, she might have been a movie star, but her parents wouldn't let her. She could have been a singer only the leader of the band wanted to sleep with her. Which she did and the rest of the band besides – and why? Because she thought so little of herself. Hmm. She could have been a model, but her parents told her she was ugly.

She could also have been a high-class hooker, fashion designer, round-the-world yachtswoman, star of the peace movement, explorer, shaman, mystic, seer, masseuse, surgeon, psychotherapist, franchisee of an American chain restaurant. Her husband had prevented all of these ambitions from coming to fruit. Oh – and she'd married her husband because he had a fast car. She had never loved him and he knew it. She was proud of that.

Now, when I heard these things, I'd cuddle her and tell her she was magnificent; she could do anything she wanted and I'd support her – hell, I'd stand and cheer.

This pleased her, and she would go on to tell me how she had fled from every oppressive disappointment – home, husband, bank manager – her long blonde hair blowing wild as a Wagnerian Rheinmaiden, her heart ripped to shreds and open to the elements, and somehow she had survived. I could picture her on a powerful white horse, or standing like Boudicca in a chariot whose wheels bristled with long deadly knives. I adored the drama of her while she was there.

And for tonight, with the pad of her thumb nudging against my clitoris, she was everything she said and more. I was in some upper circle of delirium and she was a goddess once more – to hell with Niall and his agony aunt warnings, there was stardust trailing from her heels and moonlight blazing in her eyes.

No matter that her stories contradicted each other, no matter that I'd heard of more than one ripped-off woman who'd cheerfully

lynch her; she was *grande passion cinema noir* on a good day, and even
on a bad day she made me feel like Joan of Arc.

She was also a hell of a hugger, and she had hugged me when
the sterile waste of months with Porridge had left me feeling
bruised through not being touched. Her arms had woken my tired
heart and made it worth getting up in the morning again. OK, she
didn't do a lot in bed, but after the emotional and sexual famine of
Porridge, it was wonderful that she wanted me at all, and then my
body was so hungry it would seize on any crumb and call it a feast.

When I left Porridge, I gorged myself on steamy *don't give a shit*
one-nighters, until Emilia. And only a run of too many lonely
nights without her drove me back to the bars and the likes of Chris
and Miss X and so on. I had vowed I would never be hungry that
way again. Sex is not love, but it sure feels good. And anyway,
what did the *shoop wop a doobie* hippies say – if you can't be with
the one you love, then love the one you're with. Yo, sister, yo,
brother, right on.

I paid the cabbie and held the restaurant door open by its gold
handle, shaped like a sea serpent. This was the place where TV
stars ate when they were in town. Expensive, discreet and
impressive. The sort of place where less is more and you don't ask
for ketchup. I entertained seriously rich clients here. I had
introduced Miss X to it, and she fucked me with her toes under the
crisp white tablecloth while I tongued out a lobster – just over a
week ago. We'd taxi-ed home for a night-long tour around the
Kama Sutra of her gorgeous body, and a champagne and *soixante-
neuf* breakfast. I wondered sometimes why we didn't fall in love
with each other. Maybe we were just too busy having fun.

I knew Emilia loved money flowing round her like a rising tide.
Her ex-husband and all the exes since had been mean and I did
not wish to be bracketed with them. And I got a kick out of sitting
at the toe-fuck table, and the knowing smile hovering around the
waiter's lightly rouged lips.

'If it's not on the menu, ladies,' he said, 'do just indicate what would please you and I'm sure we can improvise to your complete satisfaction. May I get you a drink?'

'Thank you,' I said, 'An Orange Blossom and a frozen margarita.'

Emilia's eyes glistened. 'You remembered,' she said, 'I feel so cherished.'

None of her exes ever remembered what she drank. So she said. I preened. Mine was the margarita – Madame had got me hooked in Hawaii, a real B-movie gringo drink for the best flying fuck she'd had, according to her.

'What sort of wine?' I asked Emilia.

'You choose,' she said, leaning towards me, spellbinding me with the glow of her eyes in the candle flame. I was transfixed. In her eyes were stars gone nova, sunshine on waves, moonrise over lakes, and my heart was a torrent of clichés.

Which wine? She was a three-bottle lush, this Emilia, and she liked red. The inflamer. And I liked what it did to her. I looked at her, this woman who held my heart tantalised over a Niagara of emotion, and saw her with a crown of daisies and harebells, bathing me in the sparkling blue of her eyes while her foot massaged mine.

'Fleurie?' I said.

'God, that's my favourite,' she said. 'How do you always know, Alex? You're amazing.'

I can lap up miles of that sort of thing, and her voice was husky and every word was a litany of love, rising as I built airy castles on the shifting sands of desire. And I knew because Emilia had told me, only she had been too pissed to remember, and I have an excellent memory, which can be useful.

We ate lobster garnished with ricks of straw-fine potato, nests of lush green watercress with cherries and strawberries glistening at the heart. Emilia's foot didn't get as high as Miss X's, but my heart roared and throbbed like a big screen orchestra from the days when Hollywood was great and Garbo. We held hands and my thumb found all the places on her palm that sent electric shocks to her cunt. She even blushed a little. Unlike Miss X, who had simply laughed as she twitched her inventive toes with an expertise that took my breath away.

I told the cab to take the river route on the way back. I was so hot and horny I wanted Emilia right now, but her ex-husband had always thought of an expensive meal as foreplay, and her other lovers – all of whom would come back to her if she snapped her fingers – had never been able to afford it. She thrived on being desired, and I wanted her own passion to build up – hell, I wanted to be ravished too.

And it worked, for when we got back to the flat and I started looking for music and a corkscrew, she grasped my hand and led me upstairs.

'Bed,' she said, 'and passion. I've been wanting you for days.'

I put the wine on the floor and let her strip me, and as she tore my silk pants to the floor and ripped sodden black lace from me, she stabbed her fingers inside me, holding my wrists as I fell against her. I lay splayed on the bed while she threw her clothes all over and flung her body onto mine. She dragged my thighs apart and shoved her whole hand against me, then stopped and lit a cigarette, which we shared while her fingers curled into my swollen lips and the heel of her hand rocked against my clitoris. She sat up and looked down on me as I came and her hand kept me coming. The moonlight turned her into a wraith and our thighs twisted almost impossibly until our cunts lay close together, throbbing and gushing. Stars spun through my mind and my body was liquid fire. From the universe of blinding orgasm, I tongue-fucked her foot and stretched my fingertips down to the raging heat of her vulva and she sagged backwards, moaning.

My turn. I wanted her to be flying with me through the rings of Saturn, floating with me in the clouds of Venus. I started to kiss her belly and held her thighs down as she arched up towards me. Each kiss was a trail of wet desire, my tongue dipping into her navel, finger and thumb kneading her nipple, until her thighs spasmed around me and drew me closer than flesh alone knows how. I slid from this grip and knelt beside her, my head diving into her belly, mouth tangled with the salt sweat of her hair, fingers teasing the hair apart, clearing the stairway to heaven that spirals around the proud mound of naked longing. The tip of my tongue hovered there and I felt the breath in her body deeper and faster.

I was spread over her like a bird landing, my arms as wings, and she took my fingers in her mouth and sucked them as my tongue explored the exploded rosebud that drew me inexorably further in. My tongue lapped around the folds of glistening hot flesh, flesh that rose like silk caught in a wild breeze around the sacred tower of her stiff and imperious clitoris. That I would ignore, until her hands plunged into my hair and I could hear her gasp for oxygen like a diver whose air lines have been cut. The smooth flesh rippled away from my tongue and her clitoris rose like Excalibur from the depths of a lake, naked and quivering like an arrow that's found its mark.

Her belly heaved; her nipples were hard and hot, and I engulfed her with my mouth, swallowed her until she filled my senses and lashed my tongue past any G-spot ever mapped.

When she came, her body was a tidal wave that swept us both from the bed, plunging me into god knows what flesh, my ears ringing with her groans and draggingly soft screams.

We slept like the drugged or the damned.

It was five when she woke me.

She was fully dressed, holding my hand lightly, whispering that she had to go. She didn't want to, but she had to. She hadn't wanted to tell me last night, since everything had been so wonderful. She'd call me to say good morning properly.

And then she was gone

I lay dazed, suddenly weeping as I heard the front door.

We'd been together for less than twelve hours.

And who the hell ever says good morning properly by phone?

Emilia – the goddamn Groke, that's who; the woman I had kidded myself I might actually Love. Left me in fucking Siberia again without a word of warning.

I sat up, tipped the wine bottle to my lips, lit a cigarette, flicked through the TV channels and watched black and white celluloid monsters eating cars and pylons. People screamed and ran, fires blazed, skyscrapers crumbled and children howled.

And so did I.

Eight

By 9 am I was fuzzy with wine and had a stack of trashy videos lined up to spend the day with. I didn't plan on anything energetic, like drawing curtains or emerging from the stale cave of my bedroom, until noon or so. I felt like a wounded animal holed up and whimpering.

Shit. No cigarettes.

The cold sunlight hurt my eyes and walking to the shop made me shaky and semi-sober. No one in the shop seemed to notice. I like my local shop. They are stingy with carrier bags, but if you buy toilet rolls, they wrap them in brown paper. God forbid anyone should know you wipe your ass!

I opened the living room windows to blow away the stale smells of booze and the last traces of her perfume. Hell, it wasn't the first time Emilia had pulled a stunt like this on me, leaving me in the small hours of the morning. It was another of her habits – like being late – that hit like a sledgehammer and made me sure that any dreams I had of Love with her were crazy. If you let a lover treat you worse than you'd take from a friend, you are seriously deranged.

Years gone past, and I'd have been playing with a pendulum, casting the Tarot over and over, rolling killer joints, trying to shake the truth from the I Ching.

Ibble ibble ibble.

Besides, I was not in love with her, I told myself fiercely.

Not unless she wanted it that way and, for god's sake, a 5 am goodbye doesn't exactly require much analysis.

Fuck it!

And tonight was a re-run with Chris and her mop of peroxide hair and her cute-enough-to-devour ass. The L word was unlikely ever to rear any of its seven deadly heads around her. I didn't even feel a flicker of enthusiasm at this dreary eleven o'clock in the morning I'd been planning to spend so differently. I had breakfast all chilled and waiting in the fridge – and then of course there was me. I should and would have been all heat and sparkle, with a zillion inventive ways of appreciating Emilia's body whirling through my brain.

I decided to purge my flat and pig out on egg and chips *chez* Mario. Breakfast with Emilia would have been avocado, smoked salmon roulade and champagne, eaten from the best plate in the universe – warm, naked flesh.

Well, there's always tomorrow. Cutie-pie Chris would be into eating and fucking – hey, tell me someone who isn't, apart from Porridge and the bloody Groke.

Breakfast with Chris?

That was a thought.

I dragged the sheets from the bed and spring-cleaned everywhere. Chris could play away tonight. Once this guy said to me *won't you stay for breakfast?* and I only realised it was a come-on three weeks later. Ah, youth! Bugger breakfast, we could play at her house or mine, anywhere, what the hell did it matter where so long as she played good and improper?

My head cleared around one, courtesy of Mario's poison-dark coffee, and I cheered up my local off-licencee by buying champagne and Greek brandy. Then an armful of lilies and stocks to turn my flat into a southern belle's boudoir. I brewed some mocha Java and rang Chris.

'You didn't miss anything at the theatre,' she grumbled. 'It was dreadful.'

I listened to her moaning for a while and made the right noises, playing elusive about how I'd spent the evening before. Chris had a good voice, a sort of acquired BBC that had been through the Gauloise/heartache mill often enough to grow a little rough and dirty, then become smooth and silky without a pause.

'So what are you planning this evening?' she said suddenly.

'Plenty,' I said. 'Would you like to eat here?'

'An invitation to Alex's lair?' She laughed, deep and filthy. 'Am I brave enough?'

'I'm just a big softie,' I told her.

Her voice went fresh as a daisy and she said that would be lovely and she'd see me at seven.

I decided to do Mexican, checking there was enough tequila for slammers. I made a Mother Hubbard inventory and then the phone rang.

'So sorry I had to go,' said the Groke, 'It's just, well, the business – and Marcie – you understand.'

'I'm trying to,' I said, my hand automatically slipping between my thighs and going straight to the spot. If she wasn't here to fuck me, I'd do it myself – and a lot better than she could be bothered to find out how.

I knew things were tough with Marcie but I was sick of hearing about it. Marcie had rung me to tell me she would kill me when I started fucking with Emilia, although Emilia had told me theirs was a purely business arrangement. There had been times I'd wanted to ring Marcie – hell, she'd been my friend well before Emilia – but whenever I mentioned this, Emilia's eyes went wild with fear and she spoke of Marcie's rages and furies and Gothic jealousy. Now, I'd never seen that side of Marcie, but I trusted the Groke to know when – if – there would be a time for that inevitable three-sided conversation.

I know different now, of course – I know the Groke will be slagging me off to whoever she's now fucking. I should send her – or him – a sympathy card. Three am blues and I even wanted to call her ex-husband and offer him my condolences.

But right now, I just kept monosyllabic and concentrated on the fresh atmosphere I'd created in honour of Chris. Then Emilia suddenly had to go – I heard a door and knew Marcie was back.

'Bye,' I said to the dull click of the phone.

Nine

Chris turned up around 7.30, done up to the nines. Lips shimmering in coral bronze, just enough mascara and kohl to underline the come-to-bed green of her eyes, cheeks shimmering with a gold-flecked soft tan. She air-kissed my cheeks and her perfume was musk and roses. Her breasts nudged mine through rose-gold silk and her thigh nudged my knee. All this was very easy on the eye and thrilled my senses; she was doing good things to me by way of lubrication and a languorous rising heat like southern sunshine.

'Nice to see you, Alex,' she said, snuggling in.

'Likewise, I'm sure,' I said.

She giggled and pecked my lips.

'A slammer?' I said, drawing away.

'Don't know what it is, but I'm saying yes,' she said.

I lit a cigarette and let it jut from my mouth as I poured an inch of tequila into both our glasses. The champagne bottle was iced with dew so I wrapped it in white linen, ripped the foil and untwisted the wire, letting the cork push to freedom in the folds of cloth.

The tequila caught the foam and I flipped the cloth round the first glass and slammed it into the table, thrust it at her and said, 'In one!'

She tossed it down, tossing her head back, arching her smooth elegant throat, then twinkling approval at me like a swimmer coming up for air.

'Different,' she said.

I slammed another for her and one for me.

'*Nostrovya!*' she said on the third. 'Or should that be, *Sayonara!* Or *Viva Zapata!* But I think we should eat. It would be all too easy and pleasant to simply get smashed and incapable.'

'Bright idea,' I said, 'let's slow it down with straight champagne.'

'You're so louche, Alex,' she purred.

'Louche?' I protested.

'Dubious, unsavoury, shady,' she said, kissing me with each word. 'It's a compliment.'

My phone rang just as she was ruining her lipstick on my earlobe. I let it ring.

'Don't leave it for me,' she said. 'I'm well aware that your elusive and possibly true love may be on the end of that line.'

'Oh, be here now,' I said, kissing her nose and she was pleased. I'd turned down the volume on the answerphone, anyway, since Emilia was very likely to snatch a few moments away from Marcie and assume I was just waiting to hear from her. Liberal and liberated though Chris liked to project herself, talking to someone else when we were getting on so well *à deux* was not my definition of good foreplay.

She sighed and shifted one thigh across the other, loading a corn chip with guacamole to feed me as the machine clicked and wound silently on. Her tongue slid across her lower lip and I leaned towards her so our lips stroked each other, teasing, tender, lighting a long slow fuse.

Chris was wearing a designer overshirt in gold and pink and a pair of silky harem pants patterned in rose. The gossamer fabric clung to her breasts. We were listening to gypsy guitars and violins, and eating burritos messily, salsa and soured cream dripping down our hands, chilli sauce adding fire to the kisses that just seemed to happen before – between – during every mouthful. I got up to pee and washed every trace of chilli from my hands with a soap that smells like a Catholic cathedral. I came back to her, turning my chair so our knees were touching.

I slipped the mother-of-pearl buttons through the fine dusky fabric of her shirt. She giggled again and raised her arm so I could loosen the wrists.

'Fists,' I said and her eyes met mine – like, *really?* She snorted with laughter and balled her hands up.

I slid the tissued sheath of gold and pink over her head and tossed it on the sofa.

'That's better,' I said. 'I intuited that you were feeling hot and I do like to make my guests – comfortable.'

'Do you have many guests, Alex?' she said, very garden party.

I wondered whether it would turn her on to think I did or did she want to play at being the only girl in the world?

'I have guests,' I said, 'only, looking at you, I can't even begin to remember who they are.'

'God,' she groaned,' That was a terrible line.'

I ran my fingertips over her bare arm and shoulder. 'That line is beautiful,' I said.

'It gets bloody worse,' she said, moving into my caress, 'Talk more shit to me, Alex, I like it.'

I sat back and looked at her. Smooth skin, her breasts held in a net of pure white lace, her gym-disciplined midriff rising and falling as she breathed. I smiled.

'Chris,' I said, 'what do you want?'

'You,' she said, reaching for the silver buttons on my baby-blue denim shirt. I caught her hand and shook my head.

'Later,' I said, and she pouted, kissing me fiercely.

We carried on eating and she kicked off her shoes. I put my foot between her thighs and she clasped it; her legs felt like steel wrapped in satin.

Finally, the table was a flotilla of Mexican wreckage. The second champagne bottle stood half-full and the third was waiting.

'Let's dance,' she said.

I stood and offered her my hand, drawing her close. Her floaty silky harem pants slid to the floor and my palms drank in the naked warmth of her, lingering on the dazzling white net around her cute ass. I rested her waist against my arm and let my other hand cup round her breast. It felt so good. Her hair was soft as warm water rippling against my cheek and my lips grazed her neck, thrilling at the pulse.

My clothes felt like armour, denim from head to foot, I felt like a homecoming military man, waltz-smooching with my girl in a precious little time, and loving every minute. I let her fumble my shirt loose and shuck it to the floor. The moment our naked flesh met was a buzz of heaven. We moved into each other, arms rolling over shoulders like waves on a shore. My breasts were naked and the feel of her tight lacy little breasts drew my nipples stiff and her belly against mine was tantalising.

She guided me to the sofa saying she was dizzy and out of breath.

'Coffee,' she said, 'before I drink any more.'

She sat cross-legged, sipping from the Chinese bowls I like to use, lapping like a cat at a saucer of cream. She put her bowl down decisively and crawled towards me on all fours. Her hair fell about her face and she kissed me, thrusting her tongue deep into my mouth, tugging at the brass Harley-Davidson buckle on my belt. I lay back and let her feel in charge for a while, a thrilling novelty after the habitual passivity of Porridge and the Groke – someone determined to do things to me.

She fought with the buttons on my jeans, the laces on my boots. I laughed and sucked my forefinger, slid my hand into her lacy panties and worked my wet finger into her beautifully tight ass. The muscles dragged over my finger as she hauled my jeans and boots away and then she snuggled into the crook of my arm.

'I need a rest,' she said.

'You're in the wrong house, baby,' I told her.

'I need a cigarette,' she said.

'Well, that's allowed,' I said.

I lit two Sobranies and gave her one, and the corny, sexually charged gesture pleased her. And me too. We blew the sweet-scented smoke around and she lodged her thumb in the silky waist of my black thong. I humped her up so my face was at her neck, and slid my finger back into her ass.

'Nice?' I asked.

'Lovely,' she said, clenching and unclenching, working into my hand so I could feel the wetness of her cunt grasping for me. I stole a little of that sweet juice and worked it around her asshole and fitted two fingers inside her.

'I've never...' she said, 'before the other night...'

'You'll like it,' I said and her dreamy green eyes gazed at me.

'You total bastard,' she murmured, 'I love it. Am I supposed to say *fuck me, fuck me now?*'

'You're not supposed to anything,' I said, concentrating on the powerful rhythm of her pulsating inner muscles. I kissed her open mouth, now swimming with desire, swallowing my tongue, sucking at my chin, lapping at my face.

'What do you want to do, Chris?' I asked her, 'Your secret fantasies are safe with me. If you like. Just tell me.'

Ten

I was sitting naked and alone on the flight of stairs that curved up to my bedroom, smoking into the darkened stairwell.

Omigosh! Did she up and leave you, oh that's terrible...

Save your sympathy – that belongs on another planet called this morning.

So where's Chris?

Take your eye round the living room, and aside from the louche debris, and a red light flashing on the answerphone, there's no sign of life. In the bathroom, only the glow of a streetlamp making ripples through the frosted glass. An occasional headlight sweeps across the walls of the stairwell, like the beam of a lighthouse. A car door slams in the street, heels clatter, screeches and growls and the bang of a door. The cute peroxide ass's metallic grey VW Beetle glitters in the lamplight.

So she hasn't gone home?

Oh no!

She is some dozen steps above me, lying on my bed.

Her wrists and ankles are tied with silk scarves. Her arms are spread wide above her head, and her legs are a wide V. Black silk blindfolds her eyes, and black silk swathes her lips to silence. The gag is only just loose enough for when she wants to talk.

All tied up and nowhere to go.

She's been there for about 45 minutes.

Her fantasy, just as she described it. My part in it was to pick the time to glide silently into the room and have sex with her without saying a word. Not one word, no matter how she begged me.

Oh – I was wearing studded wrist straps, and my hair was gelled right back from my face so I wouldn't feel like me.

The password was *Alex* – that was the game.

I was actually getting sleepy. Only the hardness of the stairs was keeping me awake. She said I was to fuck her, sleeping or waking. And then she said *please*.

After that, not a word passed between us as I tethered her, making my face a mask in the darkness.

I crept silently downstairs and drank some neat tequila. The fiery spirit ate into my throat. I lit a cigarette and smoked it through, then washed away all traces of perfume with cold water. Now I was awake.

I had decided to add a few touches of my own to her fantasy. I had a good relationship with Gavin, the sleazy guy at the adult bookshop. He said it was a relief to have a woman in who knew what she wanted without blushing, and he'd invited me into the back room to browse through the assorted erotica and stimuli saved for the serious customer. I'd indulged myself in quite a few toys and it seemed like a good time to play with some of them. After all, she'd said *anything goes*.

I padded upstairs again.

Moonlight through the skylight made a band of white across her belly, silvering her pubic hair. Her flesh rose and fell like a sand dune with something alive inside it and determined to escape. Her breasts were in deep shadow. I lit the candles I'd placed, one at each corner of the bed and sat on the floor, watching her, nudging the door with my foot when she stirred so she'd think I'd gone out again. One hand moved its fingers. Her head shifted a little.

It would be too obvious to jump on top of her. I suppressed a giggle at the thought of wardrobe-leaping and chandelier-swinging. Too obvious to touch her breasts or her cunt straight away. I thought myself into the silent night creature she wanted me to be. She'd been married, this naked creature, and she liked penetration, a word I hate, an act I adore. Screw the PC bit; Porridge had kept me out of her for years and I like to fuck as deep as is good for whoever it is.

I buckled on the slender straps of my Lady Boy, an outrageously expensive sex toy Gavin had assured me was marvellous. He said it got him hot and bothered just looking at it. It was a web of straps with a round panel where you screwed in an assortment of phallic attachments – for phallic, read longer than wide. For Chris, I chose the Big Fun Boy, a latex-covered flexible structure of titanium rods, the rods about four inches long, the whole thing about seven inches. When warm, it had the feel of flesh, unlike those hard plastic vibrators you can buy at any seaside fun shop these days. Hidden at the base of it was a hundred-hour battery the size of a thumbnail and, by nudging a concealed switch, it vibrated silently at different speeds. There was also a small tongue of latex at the base, just where it would work my clitoris. There was the inevitable penis-simulating moulding in the latex and the whole thing would have got the PC sisters up and under a banner before you could say *take me!*

Emilia didn't like sex toys, and Miss X had her own, so the Big Fun Boy was a virgin. Until now.

There was also an attachment called the Piccolo Playmate, and Gavin had thrown in a tub of lubricant, Super Up and Coming – not that he thought I needed it, he assured me, but better safe than sorry.

So I crouched at the end of my bed in this dangerous moonlight, massaging grease into the silent toy standing at my thighs. I watched Chris shift a little and kept rubbing until the Big Fun Boy and I felt warm and ready.

I took a fistful of Super Up and Coming and moved on to the bed.

Making sure I didn't touch her anywhere else, I put one hand at the base of her throat and felt her heartbeat. I caressed her neck and shoulders and played vanilla for a while, edging my other hand over her skin, slow as a cat stalking a bird. Her ass and cunt twitched as I brought my hand down on her and spread the grease around. I wiped the last of it onto her belly and felt her navel quiver.

'Talk to me,' she muttered urgently through the gag.

I had my instructions, and drew away from her entirely, kneeling back and watching her clitoris flutter in the candlelight.

'Talk to me – who are you?' she gasped.

I put my hands either side of her heaving ribs to take my weight and drew myself over her for all the world like a fool who does press-ups. I balanced on knees and one arm and drew Big Fun Boy close to her so the tip hovered just above the scarlet lips of her vulva. I let my arm return and stretched my legs and lay poised over her while she talked through the gag, begging me to speak, to tell her who I was and what I wanted.

Then I thrust Big Fun Boy deep inside her and she tried to raise her hips to meet me. The silk at her ankles kept her down and I felt the length of Big Fun Boy eat into her, gobbled up as if she was ravenous.

'Who are you, you bastard?' she hissed.

I pushed deeper and deeper into her, drew out and pushed in again slowly so I could feel every urgent breath in her body. I started to feel like Big Fun Boy was part of me, it fit so snug. I knew Chris would want me to suck her and have me play a thousand different tongue-tunes on her beautiful cunt, but I kept to the bass rhythm of fucking her till her arms were straining at their bonds. She wanted to grab me; she begged me to let her hold me, and god, it felt so wonderful in the candlelight and moonlight, I almost did.

But now I was getting into my part of the game, getting into her, I found my face stretched into a grin of delight, gazing at her thrashing head, fucking her as slow as a church bell tolls. I wanted this to last forever. Coming is wonderful but, fuck it, it's everything on the way there that's the best, once you're sure you're going to get there. Shit, I could have touched her clit and had her screaming in seconds.

So I didn't.

I felt the wet slap of her belly on mine as I thrust hard inside her. I felt the lather of sweat on her thighs as I rose and fell again.

'Really, please, untie me,' she begged.

I speeded up fucking her instead.

Then I tore the gag from her mouth with my teeth and thrust my tongue between her parted lips. I fucked her mouth in the same rhythm as my ass was pumping into her, sucked the length of her tongue and let my head dive beside hers, breathing deep into her ear, biting the lobe, bruising my teeth against the soft skin of her neck.

'Let me free,' she gasped. 'I mean it, let me free. I have to move with you.'

She sounded like she meant it, but there was no password, and I thought *no, you're my creature and I'm fucking you until you're totally mine.* I slid one hand down between our slithering bodies, her sodden hair, and pressed the tiny button. The vibration filled my belly and her hips jerked like a puppet. I pushed all the way into her, gripping her shoulders to keep me on her, for our skin was sliding with sweat and grease and the juice of sheer desire.

We were one now, every thrill tearing at her sang through my cells like an electric shock and she was moaning with near delirium and I wanted to keep her that way. I swallowed her breast and lapped her neck and she said it was too fucking much and why couldn't she just come, just fucking come, it was enough.

She started howling softly and tears spurted from under her blindfold. But still no password, so I slowed a little just to fool her.

And then I eased deep into her and fucked her and fucked her and after a while she wasn't Chris; she wasn't the cute peroxide ass – she was liquid flesh getting fucked by my liquid flesh and I felt myself suddenly become a thing of steel. My hips jackknifed against her so I was dizzy and I rammed inside her, felt her muscles grip and pull. Our skin made great sucking sounds and the waves of the ocean filled my head. I was drowning and not drowning, riding volcanic waves of heat until I melted, no bones, and lay gasping on the shore of her naked limp body, only her heartbeat letting me know she was deliriously alive.

She hadn't said what she wanted beyond this.

But I knew what I wanted.

Tenderly, I untied her wrists and ankles and rolled her gently onto her belly before I tied her again. I replaced Big Fun Boy with the Piccolo Playmate and moved so I was lying on her back, parting the fabulous curves of her ass with my fingers. More grease and I slid into the unresisting bud of her ass and fucked her until she groaned and shuddered but that didn't matter. This bit was mine, with the sweat on my belly running onto the cute cheeks of her silky ass and the baby toy rooting inside her. I grasped her breasts and fucked her until she simply didn't exist any more, only tumbling curtains of purple and green filling my head until everything went as white as staring at the sun.

She lay like the dead, and I stashed the toys for another day and went downstairs to pee.

When I came back, she seemed to be sleeping, so I smoked a cigarette while I watched her. Softly I untied her, slipped off her blindfold, and arranged myself around her.

She opened her eyes and looked at me for a long time before she sighed and smiled.

'Alex,' she said, wrapping her arms around me and kissing me so soft and light

We slept.

Eleven

Chris got up to pee around eight, and I watched the sweet curve of her back and the twin mounds of her ass as she crossed the room. Lovely. She fell back into bed and curled into my arms.

'I can hardly bloody walk,' she said.

'Does that bother you?' I asked her collarbone, nibbling the warm taut flesh.

'Oh, don't start again,' she said, ruffling her hands in my hair and drawing me close. 'I can't cope.'

That's the kind of early morning lie I like.

'Coffee?' I asked, and she said *yes, a lifesaver*, lying back on the pillows and smiling at me. I brushed her breasts with the palm of my hand as I got up and slipped into my silk kimono, a legacy from Latisha.

I slid burnished steel through the incredible softness shimmering under the crocodile skin of an avocado and made breakfast while the coffee gurgled and hissed. There were five messages on the answerphone and I ignored them. At least three would be some crap from Emilia and I was feeling too mellow to be bothered.

For Chris and her exhilarating ass, I used a deco tray and added a lily floating in a crystal dish. I took this upstairs, my body registering pleasant aches in places I didn't even know I had places.

She lay, feline and naked in the wreck of my bed, and I poured her coffee, watching her lips drink it in. She sprawled over my knees and took smooth, pale-green scoops of avocado flesh with a silver teaspoon, feeding herself, feeding me. She lay back on the pillows in the crook of my arm and smiled up at me.

'Didn't know I was getting breakfast,' she said and her green eyes sparkled.

'You're worth it,' I said, desire galvanising my muscles with slow heat.

I nudged her lips with mine, and they gave, offering her tongue, inviting mine. She licked me like a great cat. I let my hands register the sheer pleasure of her skin, lying in wait, one in the small of her back, just above the sensational curves of her ass, the other on her belly. Her spine became electric and all the soft invisible hairs clung to my fingers. Her belly pulsed against my palm.

I detached my arm from around her, and crouched over her and kissed her mouth and throat and she wrapped her arms and thighs around me.

Ah, sweet, so sweet!

We rocked together for a while until the heat wrapped us round and through. I arranged her like a doll, and she spread her arms above her head as I moved her golden thighs apart and looked down at her. I put one finger on her lips and licked and sucked it while our eyes locked until her eyelids fluttered close and her whole body relaxed.

I took one of her hands and moved down, rubbing my chin in the rough beard of her hair. Her skin shivered. I drew the lips of her cunt apart, brushing the hair aside like a fan. She spread her thighs wider and I lay down, watching her every move. I put her unresisting hand on her cunt, covered her fingers with mine, following her fingertips as she rubbed the smooth, wet, rosy purple skin, straying my thumb on hers as she moved inside.

She was expert and hard on herself, taking the tip of her clitoris between two fingers, squeezing and tugging at it until it rose, scarlet, a hard bead standing out from the mauve and lilac flesh folding around it. She rammed her hand inside herself again, her fingers emerged with gossamer strands of sweet sex – and she veiled the quivering bead in this.

She drew her knees up and the purple anemone of her asshole was throbbing. Her hand flipped over mine and pressed me close, then her hand vanished into my hair and massaged my head.

I forced her thighs down, pinning them with my arms, and brought my drooling mouth down on her. How glorious she tasted, salty, a tang of mushrooms picked at dawn, my tongue outlined every fold of skin, then I played the tip of it into the rhythmic suck and thrust of the muscle circling her inner self. I rubbed two fingertips around as she opened wider and wider, then I balled my hand into a loose fist and gave her all I could give her, right up to my wrist, and deep inside her the mouth of her womb nuzzled at my knuckles.

My mouth engulfed her clit and the wild tide of soaking naked flesh that housed it. I stroked her with the edge of my tongue, took the hard tip of her between my lips and tongue and sucked until, through the roaring in my ears, I could hear her gasping like an ocean creature that has been flung onto the shore and is dizzy for salty depths to make it free.

Her clit collapsed and she shot my fist out as if she was giving birth.

'You,' she cried. 'Now. Get here now, for chrissake!'

I slid up her body and sat with my thighs on either side of her head. Her hands had the inspired strength of ten as she drew me onto her flushed face and worked her mouth on me, licking and gorging while I rode her like a fairground horse until universes exploded in my head and my head erupted with lava and Catherine wheels dazzled and blinded me.

We lay together, like knights unhorsed in a joust where there is no victor. She muttered *Jesus!* and shuddered like she'd stuck her fingers in a live socket, and my body was a rush of seismic ripples.

We slept.

All through the day it was that way. Every time she woke, or I woke, we fucked – she fucked me, I fucked her, we fucked each other.

Early evening we shared a bath, too dazzled and high to speak much. We went out to a small restaurant near where I live and sat at a corner booth, invisible to the rest of the clientèle. We ate pasta and drank red wine, and she rallied enough on the third glass to say maybe we should make a date. Almost back to her in-control, career-woman voice.

I suggested Thursday as I pushed my hands into her lacy panties and fingered her as I talked, fucked her as she ate and poured more wine, brought her to the edge of orgasm as the waiter asked was everything all right, brought the pad of my thumb down hard on her as I poured more wine and smiled at the silent scream in her eyes and the taut muscles of her cheeks.

We walked to her car and, on the way, I pulled her into a side alley and a doorway deep in shadow. I slid her harem pants to her knees and fucked her against the door, my hand and one thigh pushing her to come over and over.

She laughed when we got to her car.

'Thursday, you bastard,' she whispered and kissed me, 'unless you want to come back tonight?'

I knew she'd say that.

'I have to work tomorrow.'

'I never asked,' she said. 'What do you do for work, Alex?'

'This and that,' I said lightly, massaging her nipple.

'Thursday, then,' she said.

I smiled and kissed her goodnight.

Twelve

What was left of the night was mine.

It was good to walk through the rooms of my flat and know no one was there, however cute and tempting their ass, however expertly bleached and curled their hair. I cherish my own company – as the song goes – but for me there have to be solid blocks of time spent with someone – some people – almost anyone will do – on either side of solitude.

Dark and late, I turn into a night owl.

Also, I guess, with no one there I'm more me than at any other time. Don't have to make with the feel-good laughter at their words, make with the fascination at their body language, don't have to ask if they want coffee, wine, music or me.

I dropped all my clothes by the washing machine. That's another blast about solitude; I can walk around naked with no reaction other than my own pleasure at the air on my skin. My feet love to be bare, my toes go aerobic with the sensation of wooden floors and carpets, even better if there's no broken glass or dog shit in a park and they can spread in the grass.

I made a cup of tea. Most of my guests don't drink tea, but it's great to wash away the stale pelt of wine and smoke. I only started smoking to break my voice into something more sophisticated. Some mornings I almost make Louis Armstrong.

I grinned to myself in the mirror.

'Alex, you bastard,' I said, 'you're looking good.'

I awarded myself fresh orange juice and tequila in a chunky-based glass. Call it sunset.

Tonight, what was left of it before the sprawling delight of sleeping single in a double bed, I would go on a trip to the Galapagos. I chose Mendelssohn's sea music to send me there.

And noticed the answerphone, now flashing seven times.

Shit.

The morning would be hectic, so I pressed play.

Emilia – the Groke – to say she loved me, did I *know* that?

Mrs Turner to confirm our am meeting which she took as confirmed if she didn't hear from me.

The Groke to say she was missing me, and wanted to just jump in her car and come see me but she just couldn't; did I understand and of course she knew I did.

Niall enquiring as to the state of my libido and liver.

Emilia – hoping I was all right and where was I, and ring her no matter how late, use our code, since Marcie was prowling the house and in tears.

The divine Miss X hoping life was treating me well, and assuring me she would treat me even better if I was free on Thursday. She had some new ideas she'd love my reaction to. The champagne was chilling as she spoke, but she certainly was not. Byeee!

I smiled and raised my glass to her as I replayed her message. Miss X could make a shopping list sound like a proposition. Thursday...hmm.

Emilia again. This time weeping because she felt *so lost* without me. I hadn't said I would be away, I should have told her, where the hell was I, *she* was on the floor. Ring her, ring her – oh – and use the code.

Our code was that I let it ring twice then hung up, then redialled. This was to avoid Marcie picking it up and giving either of us hell, although I could swear she listened on the extension half the time. Now I did and did not want to ring Emilia right now. I was feeling so chilled and up and floaty, and I knew if she was down I'd blow out Mrs Turner and everyone else just to drive through the 40% proof night to hold her through the darkness. I played all the messages through again and, goddamn it, her voice brought a familiar hypnotic tattoo to my heartbeat.

I punched the digits.

She answered on the first ring.

'I'm so relieved,' she said. 'I thought you'd crashed your car.'

'No,' I said. 'Been busy, you know how it is.'

'I didn't think you were working today,' she said. 'I've tried you all day long and last night and had to leave messages.'

'Well,' I said, 'you left a little too quickly for me to tell you what my week was like.'

'I'm sorry,' she said, 'so sorry – do you know how sorry I am?'

'Tell me,' I said, enjoying the breathy contrition.

'So sorry that I promise I'll spend the weekend with you and show you,' she said. 'I really truly promise.'

A whole weekend? I would have swooned with delight a few months before, but I'd heard these late-night promises a few too many times and sat around while they and my hopes got broken time and time over.

'I'm not sure what I'm doing,' I lied. I found if I played hard to get, she got very passionate, but the difficulty was keeping to it.

'Oh, please,' she said, 'please let me make it up to you. I feel so bad.'

Please, already!

'Well,' I said, 'I'll see how work goes tomorrow and Thursday. You know I'd love it, I really would. God knows I want you with me, but I've got a lot on.'

'Try hard for me,' she said, and started humming *the first time ever I saw your face.* Emilia can neither sing nor hum in tune, but I loved to hear her anyway. My heart lurched.

'I'll do my best,' I said, wondering for a moment why I bothered with the likes of Chris or even Miss X when Emilia could curl into my soul in seconds.

Because she's never bloody well here!

'I must let you sleep,' she said, 'my darling one. And I love you, Alex. *Te amo sempre, cara mia.* Never forget that.'

Emilia liked to remind me of her affinity with Italy – which she claimed as the home of her soul.

'Just keep reminding me,' I said. 'And I love you too.'

'Good night, *carissima,'* she said.

'Good night,' I said and cradled the receiver long after she'd hung up. Peace sat – a little uneasily – in my heart, yearning for it to be real, already I was soaring away in my mind to a whole weekend with her – did she mean Friday night, Saturday and Sunday too? God, I hoped so.

Now there was no point in ringing Miss X. Aside from my not wishing to flirt with another woman within minutes of talking to Emilia, Miss X does not like to be rung after 10.30. *The reasons, sweetie,* she said, *are manifold. One – I need my beauty sleep. Two, I need my energy and three, just suppose I were getting down and fine and funky? A phone call can ruin a crucial moment when the object of desire is dithering between sheer lust and going home.*

She was, however, great to ring in the morning and that's what I decided to do. I'd have to cancel Chris on Thursday, give her a reason that left her feeling good and willing to re-schedule.

And Niall. I'd get hold of him after Miss X and the two or three hours of Mrs Turner, and whatever half truths I shared with Chris, and just camp the afternoon away with him.

It was 1 am

I postponed tripping away to the Galapagos.

The flat was fabulously silent, and I went to bed and stretched diagonally across the whole width of it and slept like a sweet sanctified baby.

Thirteen

A lovely lascivious dream came visiting that night.

I was naked in a tangle of silky anonymous thighs, someone's hands trembling in my hair, holding my head against a gushing fountain of love juice, deaf with the sweet pressure of flesh against my ears as my tongue drank deep. My fingers were deep inside hot wet flesh, pulsing desire and pleasure. My lips were coaxing the tiny folds of a hot clit stiffer and stiffer, my tongue now hard now soft, drawing every cell to the expectation of inevitable ecstasy. I wanted and did not want to know who she was. Rainbow sparks exploded behind my sweat-soaked eyes, and I could see in the distance a pure white light; at first a dot, then a circle, then a spiral turning to lightning and striking the base of my spine, filling my shoulders as I surged into this glorious nameless woman, then forking from my tongue as the beauty pirouetting there rose against me and her distant lips howled and sang with total abandoned joy.

Then I swam up along the sweat of her body. Her thighs clamped around mine and I looked down into her face – and she was Zee, she was Miss X, for a second she was even Porridge, then she was the cute peroxide ass, and then she was Zee again. I remember thinking for a second – oh! – expecting the face to become that of the Goddess, the Groke, but it didn't. And that was OK.

And there was another face there, one I felt I knew from a long, long time back, but the impression was fleeting, like a face on a station platform as the train pulls away. A glance of green-gold eyes...and she was gone

I was wide awake around five, I guess, and lit a cigarette. My hand went between my thighs and the pool of sticky heat tangling my hair pleased me so I smiled in the pre-dawn grey and stretched like cats do, every muscle preening and purring.

The absence of Emilia from my dream bothered me slightly. But her habitual absence from my life had been bothering me for months, so nothing new there. And she had promised me this weekend, so I pushed away a sighing unease that threatened to paralyse my heart and mind.

I like waking early and taking that half hour or so to plan the day. Would be nice to have someone there awake as well, someone to make tea, to make tea for, someone to smile back at me and make lazy, wake-up love with. Well, I would just have to do, so I made me come in waves of well-travelled, head-to-toe dizziness, then I stumbled downstairs and made tea for me, coming again as I leaned against the door.

I ran a bath and lay in foam-scented luxury.

First thing this morning I'd have to be in business mode. I have a series of suits for this. Pinstripe, lilac, scarlet, white, powder-blue and navy, depending on the client, depending on the property, depending at what stage we are at as I discover exactly what they are wanting their houses to say about themselves, who they are wanting to impress and just how much they are willing to spend in the process. After that, it's up to me to find the furniture, the wall coverings, the ornaments, the carpets, the rugs. It's like setting a stage where the actors are amateur and the script is improvised snobbery or family drama. I was amazed to create this job, to find people who really don't know what to put in their own homes, and who will pay me vast sums of money to go shopping for them. It's a peach of a job and, for me, the best thing is I can put in as much or as little time as I want. And I'm good at it – I never repeat a room in the slightest detail. Too many of my clients know each other.

Mrs Turner was a rich bitch, neurotic about her decent terraced roots, married in heavy gold rings and chains and bracelets to George, a property magnate, whose Yorkshire vowels broadened with success, while hers had been elocuted to near-extinction. I had a feeling I would have liked her as she was before the millions, for there was one time when she almost relaxed into being herself, perched on the chrome-ringed bar stools of her immaculate kitchen. We were drinking tea. She was talking and I was listening. Listening, listening, knowing the bar stools would be going, the pull-down light would be consigned to history, the gleaming cold grey floor was out. Because Mrs Turner liked cooking and she and Ken liked to eat in the kitchen on the rare evenings that business allowed them any evening together. As she was now, Mrs Turner amused me. Today, we would get on first name terms, I knew, and after that I would be her best friend until her house was transformed. She'd had the pinstripe, and the navy. Today would be powder-blue, the mummy-granny colour that worked every time. Like a dream.

It would be OK to ring Miss X in an hour or so. She always woke around six to start her regime of keeping young and beautiful, with exercises that tightened her pelvic floor and stomach, then twenty minutes of steam to drain every pore of any trace of grime, then a bowl of crushed ice that left her breasts tingling and taut, a fruit-smelling scrub that annihilated cellulite, then a viscous green goo to thicken her hair while volcanic mud smoothed any wisp of a line from her face and neck. When I stayed with her, I helped her skip the exercises and joined her in the steam, and then she would scream at me to stop laughing or the mud would crack. I wondered what she had planned for Thursday. Whatever it was, it would be fun.

And the cute peroxide ass. Hmm. Dear Chris. I'd played it so she wanted me again, and wondered how to blow out Thursday so she'd be wanting me more. That's the hard bit with playing games

– she might be sitting in her office later today wondering if Thursday was a good idea once she'd coffee-ed herself sober and awake.

I dried off, listening to Mozart, my music for an efficient day.

7.13.

Time to filter coffee and start with clothes. Mrs Turner noticed such things, and I wouldn't have been surprised to find her wearing hers inside out so people could be sure of noticing the designer labels and judge her the way she wanted them to. When people are born with money, they can dress like tramps and be treated like lords. When they acquire oodles of the stuff, their minds are still bargain hunting and anxious about bills and proud of an economy that is no longer necessary and it doesn't matter if it's Armani or Gucci or DKNY, they are as nervous as an actor on a first night that lasts most of their lives. They've made it, they've made it, but body language and darting eyes question what exactly it is they've made. It's OK for the children – for children everything around them is the way it's always been, and they sulk and waste and pout at talk of hard times or anything being other than taken for granted. Mrs Turner had one son who had a degree, and she was astonished that this marvellous achievement had become ordinary in the moneyed world her husband's work had bought for them. She'd said she wanted to make a cake for him, and that's when I warmed to her. It was such a little wish, to make your son a cake for his achievement after years of helpless anxiety to assure his place in a better world. But success had bought him that world when he was pre-school and Mrs Turner's home-iced cake became a party catered for by strangers where she flitted nervously from guest to guest, feeling tolerated and patronised in her own home. I would do Mrs Turner's place but *good*. It only takes a spark of humanity to light my enthusiasm. Whatever she said now, I would always see her standing in her kitchen, looking at the virginal mixing bowl, reaching out for an immaculate steel spoon, then letting her be-ringed hand drop, useless, against her cashmere skirt.

I sprawled on the sofa, cream lace cupping my breasts, a cream silk thong riding my hips and dialled the – by now – deodorised and all but genetically modified Miss X.

Fourteen

'Darling,' she said, 'how very nice. I'm just about to decant some Blue Mountain and raise my drug levels. Give me just *one* moment.'

I heard the rustle of silk, the clatter of a heavy crystal ashtray, the burst of steam from her chrome coffee machine. Then the sound of a chair on the pale bare boards of her floor and she was back with me.

'What's Thursday?' I said.

'A window in my week, Alex,' she said, and her lighter flicked, 'a week of business suits and funding. and I'll go mad if I don't do something very me in it all. It seemed to me that we could share the pleasure. If you like. If that love of yours isn't dropping by.'

Miss X was lightly sarcastic about the Goddess/Groke. Lightly and briefly, where Niall had to be told to simply leave it alone.

'Sounds lovely,' I said.

'I thought I'd cook,' she said, 'just to line the stomach. And then we can simply play, darling. I shall be up at some vile hour of Friday morning, that's the only interruption.'

'What sort of time?' I said.

'I'll be back for six,' she said, 'but whenever. It's always nice if you're here already...'

Miss X had this burglar fantasy, assisted by the way her door key lived under a gargoyle at her back door.

'That's fine,' I said. 'Don't know what time I'll be there.'

'OK,' she said and her breath exhaled smoke and slowed the two sounds with a shivering expectation I knew very well.

'Are you alone?' we said together.

Then *yes.*

'What are you wearing?' I asked her.

'I'm wearing my silk robe,' she said, and giggled. 'I was wearing my silk robe. It is now on the floor. And you?'

'Cream silk bra, cream silk thong,' I said. 'I'm on the couch.'

''I'm sitting at the table,' she said.

'Put your hand on your right breast,' I told her. 'Now. Just cup your hand there, then rub your nipple between your thumb and forefinger.'

'OK,' she said. 'What are you doing?'

'I'm standing on the other side of the room,' I said, 'watching you. But you don't know I'm there.'

'OK,' she said, 'my nipple is getting really hard.'

'Fleur,' I said, 'you can just hear the creak of leather. Slide your hand down to your navel and spread your fingers so they just touch your hair.'

'Nice,' she said, 'and you?'

'Bugger me,' I said. 'Just start to move your thighs apart, just stroke them with your fingertips and start to move your ass forward and back a little until you feel wet.'

I heard the chair move a little and Fleur's breath thicken.

'OK,' I said, 'now stroke the hair between your legs with one finger, really slow and hard, slow and hard and slide your finger down into the cheeks of your ass. And tell me how it feels.'

'Wet, Alex,' she whispered, 'wet and hot.'

'I'm moving towards you now, from behind,' I said. 'You know I'm there but you haven't seen me yet. You can feel the heat of my body at your back.'

'Yeah,' she said and her voice was shaking.

'I'm coming to face you,' I said, picturing her quivering body. 'I'm putting my hands on your knees and pushing them wider and wider apart.'

'In leather?' she said.

'In gauntlets,' I said, 'You can't see my face for the visor. My hand is on your wrist and I'm pushing your fingers into your cunt. There's a leather grip on your wrist and I'm moving you in, deeper and deeper.'

'Fuck you!' she gasped.

'No,' I said and made my voice harsh, 'fuck *you*, while I watch your face.'

I listened to her gasp and the chair creaking and saw her in front of me, neck taut and mouth open.

'You're sliding to the floor,' I said, 'and I'm standing over you watching you. Put your hands over your head.'

'Fuck me,' she said. 'Jesus, just fuck me.'

'That's your job,' I said, 'Move your ass up and down, grind your ass into the floor. And keep your hands still.'

'God!' she said, and I could hear her flesh against the polished wood.

'Move your hands down now,' I said, 'one between your thighs, one on your face – suck your fingers hard and work at your beautiful cunt till you come. I'm kneeling between your legs, watching your every move.'

The phone clattered to the floor and I heard her groans and gasps, while I lit another cigarette, waiting for the siren wail that was Fleur flying into shuddering orgasm. It came and her fist thumped the floor. I saw her tossing her whole body from side to side. Then heard a clatter as she picked up the phone.

'Well,' she said, 'good morning to you, Alex. That was wonderful.'

'My pleasure,' I said, smiling. 'So what are you doing today?'

'Reeking of sex, dear heart,' she said, 'I shall fly through the day with a healthy glow on my face and a tingle in all the right places. And you?'

'Client,' I said, 'Yorkshire business magnate's wife.'

'And is she...?'

'Fleur, please!' I said. 'You know clients are off limit. I only mix pleasure with pleasure.'

'Do you now?' She laughed.

You see, I met Fleur when she wanted her house done. I had been recommended to her by the Greek shipping aristocrat whose English home was a few drives away from hers. Only Fleur's house was perfect just the way it was, and that we decided within an hour. Perfectly icy too was the bottle of Saumur she opened, and the Deco flutes she poured it into. So we had dinner instead and, too drunk to drive home, I slept in her studio spare room until the early hours when she decided to join me – *For a cigarette at least, Alex*, she said.

I thought I was a gay experiment for her, since everything about Fleur is modelled to please the male sex. As our *affaire* progressed, I learnt that she swings both ways and makes no apologies. I think she tells the girls, but not the boys, but hell, it's none of my business.

'So is Thursday fine with you?' she said, as I heard the snap of her lighter, 'or *is* that love of your life dropping in – I do understand, you know.'

I laughed. One of the things I like about Fleur is her complete avoidance of the big L word in connection with me. Feels safe that way – also her detailed fantasies, like the motorbike courier one we had just acted out – her many scenarios usually demand anonymity, which is why I call her Miss X. I dithered for a second – and felt the tug of the familiar pull me.

'Thursday is cool, man,' I said.

'I will cook,' she said. 'You can pour drinks. A nice evening at home, if that suits you?'

'A quiet evening in front of the telly, dear,' I said.

'You're very intuitive,' she said. 'I've been having some alterations done in the attic, Alex.'

'Yeah? What?'

'You'll like them,' she said, and refused to say more.

Knowing Fleur, *alterations* could be anything at all. The last time she'd used the word, it had been iron rings screwed into the wall above her bed – and what fun that was.

Time to go and see Mrs Turner and still too early to ring Chris.

I put on my powder-blue trousers and tucked in an ivory crêpe de chine mandarin blouse. The jacket had a Deco silver wreath glistening with real pearls on the lapel. My shoes were dull silver too, hand-stitched. They cost me a small fortune, but the whole look earned me more than its weight in gold.

These days, I was driving a black Alfa Romeo sports convertible whose numberplate happened to coincide with my initials. Only Fleur knew that this was mere coincidence and she thought it was very chic. And funny. She said it was just like me. She'd bought me black, Italian leather driving gloves which, she said, I could use in the car as well. I slipped them on and thought of the feel of her breasts through their soft black fingers and on my naked palm. Definitely leather this Thursday – unless she requested otherwise.

With that thought, I stop-started through the suburban traffic and cut across onto the flyover leading to the motorway. Mrs Turner was some forty miles away, so I relaxed to Mozart and blew smoke out into the open air.

Fifteen

On the road to Mrs Turner's it was not unusual to be shadowed by a Rolls Royce or BMW or some other beautiful monster that blatantly screams of material success. Today, it was a daffodil-yellow Porsche Carrera that seemed determined to hump the neat black ass of my car. The road switchbacked through ancient tunnels of trees, sunlight dappling the road with leopard spots of inky black. Wide, rolling meadows spread as far as you could see, their lush green, sheep-studded acres a sign of the estate that covered half the county. The Porsche driver irritated the hell out of me; this was a lovely road, every turn brought natural beauty no matter what the season, and I had to be super calm knowing the state of Mrs Turner's nervous system.

Three more bends would find me at a hump-backed bridge where I could pull over and watch the river flow for a while, so I did. The balding bucolic driver behind me tore past, within an inch of me. I waved to him – whether he saw or not was irrelevant. My irritation vanished with the gesture. Only seconds later, the whole place spoke peace. The sound of the river was music enough, that and the breeze in the heavy oak branches dipping down beside the clear water.

I sat on the old stone wall and lit a cigarette, watching the blue smoke tug away and vanish upstream. This was a dream of mine, to live in a place where the view was only green and more green and the most exciting thing was the slow grey flap of a heron, or the splash of an otter. It's a fantasy I have yet to share with anyone. Because, of course, for it to be perfect, there would be someone else there who dreamed the same dreams and wanted to share them with me. Someone who would be all to me, and I all to her. Someone to come home to, to come home with, someone to find rivers and waterfalls with. Someone who would go to sleep holding me and be there when we woke in each other's arms. That's what I wanted more than anything else in this world. The elusive – no, mythical! – Ms Right.

I realised with surprise that I had never even considered sharing it with the Goddess. Maybe because she'd never asked me, and even making plans for an evening or weekend around me seemed to provide her with incredible trauma.

And all my *affaires* had been urban – so far, apart from the time I'd spent with Jodie. I was in a city when I realised it was women for me – or did I realise it was women for me and go to the city? Maybe a bit of both. Only in a city can you find a community of gay people – our own bars, cafés, nightclubs and even shops. Whole colonies – years ago, Zee's entire street was gay squats. But if being gay is all you have in common, it does not necessarily make you friends or even good neighbours – as I found out when I squatted in Zee's basement. The city gives you places where you can hold hands and smooch and dance and flirt without anyone laying their tight-arsed prejudices on you. And if anyone did, well, in those days you had an army of your own kind to protect you, and a hundred doors open to you – a proud and glad underground. These days being gay is a bold and fashionable statement – every home and soap opera should have one, or at least know *someone like that.* 'Glad to be gay' is simply a statement these days, where once it was a defiant battle-cry.

I looked over the wall into the river where sunshine made silvered elastic jigsaw shapes of the moving surface before they vanished in a band of shadow under the bridge. And I knew that, one day, there would be a she who'd be happy with just me and a view from the window of green hills and the sea, and evenings sipping wine in a green dusk while the hills became smoky blue and the moon silvered a path across the waves. I refused to disbelieve in Love and I also refused to be alone. I guess that's why there was the Goddess – and Fleur and Chris and whoever else wished to come and play with me.

Chris. I should ring her before I got to Mrs Turner's. It's a good idea to have phonecalls sometimes when I'm working; I even set them up sometimes to give the impression of how valuable my time is. But Mrs Turner needed one thing from me that no one else had ever given her – apart from her son when he was helpless and needed her. Mrs Turner needed, and would have, my undivided attention.

I got Chris's switchboard.

'May I enquire what it's concerning?' asked the bright-voiced operator.

I hate that.

'No,' I said, 'just tell her Alex.'

'Chris Lawrence,' Chris eventually answered, office-efficient.

'Hi, Chris,' I said. 'How are you this bright and sunny morning?'

'Oh, don't be so cheerful,' she said. 'It's pouring with rain and my hangover stinks. The girls dropped by last night, I think to get the dirt on you. So I got them drunk instead, and then I couldn't let them drink alone.'

'Dirt?' I said.

'Yes,' Chris said, 'they are all agog. Don't worry, I was enigmatic. The Sphinx would have been proud of me. And what do you mean, bright and sunny? It's pouring with rain here. Where are you?'

'Halfway across the country,' I half-lied. 'Work. I have a new project in the middle of the countryside. It's beautiful here.'

'You and the countryside don't fit together – in my mind,' she said. 'You're city, Alex, don't kid yourself. And this new project, what is it? Or who is she?'

'Mrs Turner. Fulfilling her fantasies,' I paused and lit another cigarette then finished, 'in the context of a rather grand house.'

'Bitch!' said Chris, laughing. 'What are you really doing?

'Just that,' I said, 'fixtures and fittings and *objets d'art*.'

'So I suppose Thursday's out?' Chris asked, sounding scathing.

'I hope not,' I said, 'I won't actually know until later and it's possible I'll be back. But it is a large house and she is a very fussy woman, and she's in a hurry. I'm going to have to work miracles.'

'Well, that's good in a way,' Chris said, 'because Thursday's hopeless for me. I've got a meeting with some wretched fundraiser all afternoon and it may drag on until evening. One of those bloody awful businesswomen with balls. Let's find another time, shall we?'

'Yeah,' I said. 'Shall I ring you – or do you want to do that now?'

We decided Wednesday next week.

'Anyway,' I said, 'a businesswoman with balls might be quite fun.'

'You don't know this one,' she said. 'Fleur O'Brien. She's a monster.'

I stopped myself laughing. Fleur O'Brien? There could hardly be two.

'Where's she from?' I asked.

'Oh, some urban redevelopment corporation,' Chris said. 'She'll be one of those iron-grey-haired women with big asses in suits, made up like a third-rate drag act, I expect. The sort of woman who's never had a good shag in her life and is probably gay, anyway, only too stupid to realise it. Sister George. Gets off on money and power. She's very high up.'

Well, well, Chris, you're in for a surprise, I thought. Fleur would tell me all about it on Thursday night and I looked forward to that in a voyeuristic way.

'So, Wednesday then, Chris,' I said. 'Should we go out? Stay in? Both?'

'Yes,' she said. 'Play it by ear. Ring me. And good luck with – who is it?'

'Mrs Turner,' I said, 'Turner's Steel and Plastic Coatings. Built to Last. Protect and survive. You Know it Makes Sense.'

'*That* Turner,' Chris said. 'I am impressed. Didn't know you moved in such circles.'

'Ah, but I do,' I said – god, you could almost hear Chris's wheels turning – Turner, money, funding – 'and I'd better go. Can't keep a lady waiting.'

'Remember that on Wednesday,' she said, suddenly husky.

'I will,' I said, letting myself go a little husky too.

Sixteen

I gained access to Mrs Turner's drive when the security video intercom allowed the wrought-iron gates to swing wide open soundlessly. I drove past the heavy twirls and spikes, monogrammed with the Turner initials and a crest gleaming in gold. My wheels crunched on raked gravel for a quarter of a mile, and I parked in front of the wide stone steps where Mr Turner wanted to set his initials and crest in brass – and I hoped I could persuade him away from this idea. It made me think of Victorian seaside hotels and would jar with the soft grey stone.

The house had been built as the country seat of a minor eighteenth-century peer, then a nineteenth-century politician used it for his mistress and children and after that the Great War had seen it nursing shell-shocked soldiers back to reality. A pop star took it over for a while but abandoned it when the authorities refused him a heli-pad.

And now the Turners were in residence, determined to make their mark.

Nothing had been allowed to alter the elegant exterior and little had changed inside, apart from the pop star adding a swimming pool tiled with the face of Elvis Presley, with a Jacuzzi set on his famous quiff like a halo. It was fabulously vulgar, bordered by gorgeous malachite tiles, and I knew Mrs Turner wanted rid of the whole thing, saying she found green depressing. I planned to talk her out of this but I'd have to work out her overall effect before I'd know how.

That's the bit that fascinates me with really wealthy people. So much of it is to impress – more, to make a particular impression on a particular group of similarly wealthy people. One billionaire couple I worked for didn't even live in the main part of the house they'd spent a fortune on – they had a tiny flat and kitchenette at the back where everything was instant coffee, microwave dinners and MFI. They felt more comfortable there than in the petrified forest of heavily insured antiques they had me find for them. To their coterie of non-friends, they pretended that the back flat was for the staff.

My job was to find out what each room was really for and, more importantly, who. If I can find that out and get an idea of colour, then the rest is easy. Over the years I've built up contacts with a plethora of artists and craftspeople who can produce almost anything in any material, so that I can guarantee my clients that their décor is unique. That's the one thing they all have in common: their wealth should buy them something that no one else has ever seen or owned – unless it's antiques and then there has to be a platinum-edged pedigree. My antique dealers are a bunch of rogues and queens who enjoy the game as much as I do.

Mrs Turner's butler met me at the door. He was an excessively handsome young man and Mr Turner called him his wife's toyboy, which she found embarrassing. He had one of those acquired accents which lacerates vowels in the manner of Lloyd Grossman, and his expressions were a parody of the latest TV parody of Jeeves. I felt that the anonymity and remoteness of the Turners' country retreat suited him – he had the air of one on whom a suit sits uncomfortably, like a bouncer.

'Whom shall I say to madam is here?' he asked loftily.

'Alex Scott,' I said. 'Mrs Turner is expecting me.'

I waited for her in the drawing room, which was cream and gold in an expensive but faded way, like a country house opened to the public through financial desperation. The chair legs twirled, the curtains swagged dustily, a large oval table ruined the curve of the bay windows. Two large landscapes sagged in heavy sculpted frames, and a brash portrait of Mr Turner topped the elegant fireplace in a modern frame of almost the same design. Occasional tables stood here and there, one with a copy of *House and Garden*, another with a chess game half-played – the pieces were in the same places as when I had last visited. One table had a plate-glass top supported by a rather clumsy dolphin. A wide-screen TV blocked the bottom half of the beautiful mother-of-pearl inlay of a huge cabinet. There was a tapestry on one wall, vaguely heraldic with a hunting scene. Most of the pieces in the room were rather fine, but put together, the effect was that of a warehouse.

I heard Mrs Turner's nervous stilettoes in the hall, and in came the lady herself, clad in taupe from head to foot, her cashmere sweater pulled sideways by an over-large brooch, antique gold top-heavy with pearls forming a bunch of grapes. It had belonged to the Duchess of Windsor and she always wore it, terrified of losing something so costly. Her apricot lips stretched into a smile.

'Miss Scott,' she said, 'will you have a cup of tea?'

'Alex, please,' I said. 'I'd love a coffee.'

Now, she was dithering. Should she ring the bell, since I was somehow a tradesperson, or should she go herself? She darted at the bell pull and perched on the brocade sofa opposite.

'I feel I must have got you all confused,' she said suddenly, 'when you last came. There's so much to be done, you see, and George – Mr Turner – says it's all up to me. There's a lot of entertaining, you see, Alex, and I look round and I can get an idea of a room – then it just seems to be a corner. Like this room. I bought that table last week; it looked lovely when I saw it, but I don't like it now.'

'It's a beautiful table,' I said, 'and don't worry about a thing. That's my job. And you didn't confuse me, Mrs Turner. I've been doing this for years and so far I've had no complaints. I think the thing is to take one room at a time and look at everything everywhere. And if we can't find the right sort of things, then we can have them made.'

She sighed and frowned.

'I wish I had your confidence,' she said, 'and do call me Marjorie.'

'Well,' I said, 'all I need you to do is tell me where you want to start. My time is yours.'

The housekeeper brought in a tray, fussy cups and silver pots, and Marjorie relaxed as she poured out tea and coffee.

'Well, what about this room?' she asked. 'Why don't we start here? I spend quite a bit of time in here, you see, and then we tend to come in here after a dinner party. So there have to be lots of seats, you see.'

'We need to see this room empty,' I said, 'not shift the furniture, but see how it would be starting from scratch. I need to know which pieces you like and the sort of colours that you like. I can take notes while you're talking and do you some sketches. So you sit in here – and then there're your guests; anything else happen in here?'

'I do needlepoint,' she said, her face relaxing. 'George likes his telly. When Hugh come home, he likes a game of chess. I don't play it, but he and his father, well, they've always played chess. Our guests have their coffee or drinks.'

'Needlepoint?' I said, wanting to pull her back to that point of relaxation, 'I have an auntie who does that.'

Auntie Niall, queen of Islington Green, he of the acid tongue, she of the bee-stung lips and scarlet crinoline...

'Shall I show you?' she said, rising and opening the Queen Anne escritoire. She crossed over to me with an armful of her work and, as she sat beside me, I smelt Chanel No. 5. Her face was animated as she handed me her work – flowers and kittens and cottage gardens.

'Lovely,' I said. 'How you have the patience!'

'I've always loved needlework,' she said, 'invisible mending,

Alex, it kept us fed many a time before George made his fortune. And it's not just patience, it's time. God knows I've got plenty of that.'

I made a mental note: fussy and flowery and needing to be busy.

'But that doesn't help with this room,' she said, sweeping up her work.

'Just spread them out on the table,' I said. 'Helps me get a feel of what you like.'

'I want a piano,' she said suddenly. 'I used to play, you know. Mother played the organ at the Chapel, and music lessons, well, that's paid the bills on more than one occasion. A very long time ago.'

'This room would take a grand piano,' I said, and she smiled. I knew exactly where her piano was as well. Tim Smallboy had been on the phone only last week, crowing about the bankrupt stock of a disgraced rock musician, and giving me first refusal.

'I think chairs should be comfy,' she said, her eyes glittering. 'It's not just what they look like, is it? George likes these things, very proud of them, but I don't notice him sitting in them. And what's a chair for?'

'You can have both,' I said, 'looks and comfort. It's just the style that's the problem. I've got catalogues to get an idea.'

She relaxed with the pile of glossies I gave her which gave me a chance to survey the room. A piano...a soft damask background, needlepoint cushions, a mirror to reflect the bay window, a repro cabinet for the monster TV in a corner of the room arranged for family, even if family was seldom there. At the moment, the room was carpeted in a whiter shade of beige, yellowed by the skirting boards, but I knew the boards beneath would be an immaculate pale gold and that rugs were the thing. Powder blue, soft rose, cream – the whole effect would be restful and classic, in fact too restful for George's need for grandeur. Nothing could be decided until Marjorie Turner settled on furniture. At one point when white carpets, marble onyx and gold were all the rage, I called it gilt and snot, and knew that George would go for the gilt in a big way. It would distract from the brash colours of his portrait, which I really wanted to evict to the hall. And the landscapes were in as desperate need of cleaning as a pub ceiling, for under that brown film lay cobalt-blue skies and a spring green in the trees that modern paint simply cannot capture.

'Ooh,' she said, 'what about these?' She was very excited as she showed me the picture. 'That's what I call classy.'

'It certainly is, Marjorie,' I said.

Seventeen

'White leather sofas,' I said to Fleur's nipples as she giggled about Mrs Turner. 'Rococo standard lamps with white lotus uplighter shades.'

She tugged my hair and drew my face up to hers, stabbing my mouth with her tongue. Her naked thighs were locked around my tight leather jeans and she ground her hips and belly against the heavy silver belt buckle.

'Talk filthy to me,' she said. 'What about the floor?'

Fleur had a thing about fucking on the floor. And against a door. And tables do something to her too, perched on the edge with her inner thighs sticky and hot against my face. She went very assertive when we did land up in bed and that was a blast, the silky weight of her pinning me down...

But floors were her favourite, and words like parquet, quarry tiles, broadloom, – even Axminster – could send her body into a frenzy of clawing passion. I had never tried whispering sweet lino to her and I wondered about that – maybe during one of her rough trade fantasies? Coconut matting? Drugget? We'd no doubt see.

I smiled as I bit her neck gently and tongued her ear.

'Very pale oak boards,' I whispered and felt her arch her back. 'Going to be Chinese rugs, but they have to be authentic and spotlessly antique. Solid legs on the lovely white leather sofas – all the better to tie you to, my dear. You should feel the smooth grain of the wood on your spine.'

'Go back to *tie me to*,' she said urgently. 'The radiator's solid. I think, darling, we can forget about the table.'

One time when Fleur and I had fucked, she wound up dragging

the table over with the leather thongs binding her wrists. It was after that that she had the iron rings bolted into her bedroom wall. I crouched over her, shoved my thigh against her wet cunt and pushed her nearer the wall. Tying her wrists to the radiator felt good as she struggled and tossed her head from side to side, and called me bastard.

I sat astride her shaking body and looked into her flushed face, then leaned forward to kiss her wet lips, and tie a silk gag over her mouth.

'Mirrors,' I said. 'Either side of you and above us, all around.'

I knelt on one knee, the other keeping her thighs apart and slipped the buckle of my belt, drawing the silver links slowly across her breasts. I untied the lace of my jeans and stroked her belly with the rough cord. Her skin was a sheen of sweat and I slid the leather down my legs, drawing its hard smoothness along her thighs. My hand ruffled the luxuriant curls of hair that made a red-gold V and I felt a demanding hot pulse raging through her. Fleur comes in seconds the first time and then I can really start to play, so I stood and kicked my jeans away, then knelt swiftly and brought my mouth down on her hot, pulsing clit and stiffened my tongue at the quivering base, drawing the tip upwards and engulfing the hard bud with my lips. Fleur's thighs thrashed as the gag muffled her screams of ecstasy and her body shuddered head to foot before she went completely limp.

I untied her gag and buried my lips in hers, teasing her lower lip, rubbing the tip of my tongue against her teeth, sucking her lovely tongue. Her eyes sparkled and she snuggled against me.

'I want my hands back,' she said.

'Beg me,' I said.

'I'm telling you,' she said, laughing wickedly, 'or you won't be able to come up and see my attic. And, dear heart, believe me, it's designed with you in mind.'

I nuzzled her neck.

'And I want to feed you,' she said. 'You're going to need all your energy, believe me.'

'Mm,' I said, tracing the hollow at the base of her neck and working down to her breasts. Fleur thought her breasts were too small, but I thought they were perfect. Mind, I have never met a breast I didn't like. Except once in LA and that was Randy the raven-haired lap dancer with a silicone job and nipples perfectly and permanently erect, and that felt weird.

'No point playing with them babies,' she told me. 'Can't feel a fucking thing since the job, but hell, they pay the rent.'

Fleur's breasts were alive and firm. Her nipples were dark pink and completely smooth until I massaged them between thumb and finger or drew my teeth gently over the moth-wing aureole of soft skin, when they hardened into huge, damson points and licking them very lightly made her whole body quiver and start like a jolt of electricity had shot through every cell. Right now, her nipples nudged against my teeth and she writhed like a cat in the sunshine.

'This is an order,' she said huskily. 'Unless you have some golden rain fantasy, give me my fucking hands back. Oh, please, pretty goddamn please, Alex, I have to pee. OK, bitch, I'm begging you.'

I sat back and untied her and watched as she ran out of the room. The peachy curves of her ass with a deep shadow in the cleft and a dimple either side of the base of her spine – and a pink suggestion of wood grain on her skin, her smooth tanned legs...Fleur was very easy on the eye whichever way I looked at her.

I poured us some wine, red for me, white for her. Smoky Rioja and Chablis chilled to polar perfection. Then her arm slid round my waist and I felt her body melt into my back. She had crept up on me like a shadow and her hand drummed lightly on my belly, then slid like an eel between my thighs. She nudged my thighs apart with her knee and her hand snaked round to my ass, smooth fingers rubbing deep between the cheeks. The weight of her body pushed me forward over the breakfast bar, and her hand slid against my soaking cunt. Fingers worked inside me, deep and fast, and she ground her hips into my ass. The rhythm got faster and faster and I groaned as my legs shuddered, becoming liquid foam. Now her fingers worked over my clit and delirious ecstasy filled me in volcanic waves.

'You're not coming yet,' she whispered fiercely. 'You're not coming yet, you're not...'

And on and on in a throaty growl, the words beating in time with her flying fingers.

My body went into orbit and I collapsed to the floor, where she wrapped herself round me, and I held onto her like a woman drowning while a tidal wave ripped through me, tossing me around like an abandoned skiff. Her hand smoothed my hair, and wiped sweat from my eyes, then her mouth butterflied all over my face. Her touch was so tender I could have cried.

'How was it for you, darling?' she said, laughing, Fleur again, sounding all in charge and brisk with dinner on her mind.

'Not bad,' I said, my eyes still closed, loving the soft heat of her and the way my body seemed to have lost all its bones.

'I'm going to help you totter to a chair, Alex,' she said, 'and be the naked chef, Delia Smith off-camera.'

I sprawled with my glass of wine and lit a cigarette, watching her chop and skewer and toss a rainbow of salad and exotic vegetables. Fleur did international cuisine with an almost complete absence of calories: she was fanatically slender and had said she had to eat nothing to balance out the booze which she drank with the panache of Joan Collins' Alexis.

Suddenly she looked up at me and put down the Viner's knife. She raised her glass and smiled radiantly.

'Alex,' she said, 'that was lovely, dear heart. I just wanted to tell you. Absolutely drop fucking dead wonderful. Thank you.'

'My pleasure,' I said, raising my glass to her.

It was unusual for Fleur to say anything like that and I was puzzled. It felt close to the edge of our pact never to mention the L word, but it felt OK. Like the tender moments when she had been holding me in her arms. And I guess I loved Fleur, but maybe we had too much fun together to have it threatened by straying into the minefield of emotions.

She smiled again and picked up her knife.

'I had a meeting today,' she said. 'It was rather odd. Can I tell you about it? You might make sense of it.'

'Go ahead,' I said.

'It was strange,' she said. 'It's the part of my job where I recommend projects and schemes for grants and bloody Laurel and Hardy were there – why do I have to work with fossils? I feel like God, sometimes, Alex, and wicked bitch that I am, I love it. So there I was – you know my linen suit? The one that makes you laugh? Yes? The lah di dah business lady one?'

'I know the suit,' I said, running my tongue over my upper lip as she looked at me. I had grabbed her once as she came in from work wearing it and she fought me fiercely, saying the damn thing creased too easily.

'You are not going to ruin it,' she said now, laughing.

'One day,' I said, 'one day, wear it for me, darling. I too have fantasies.'

'All right,' she said, 'I'll surprise you.'

'Darling, you always do,' I told her. 'What about this meeting?'

She grated ginger and it amazed me the way her perfect nails seemed to retract like a cat's claws.

'I was sitting there, Alex, you know, behind the executive desk, thinking of you, actually. Feeling quite mellow and this meeting started. Laurel and Hardy in their dreadful suits and this woman came in and, god, she was aggressive. Felt like she hated me, my love, and it was rather uncomfortable. She had her outlines and plans in a folder, very efficient and reasonable and I was in rubber-stamp mode, but she put my back up. Sarky comments about grant-givers and a lot of guff about worthy sections of the community. As if she were lecturing an ignoramus and, darling, I would hardly be under-selling my mucky little soul in this job if I didn't know all that. I mean, would I?'

For all Fleur came on like a diamante Sherman tank, she genuinely cared about her work and had a way of charming people.

'She was vile,' she said, 'lovely to Laurel and Hardy and then all power-bitch with me!'

'You should have thrown her out,' I said.

'That's the trouble,' she said. 'For all she was being really rather nasty – and I didn't and don't know why, I kept looking at her and you know, darling, I really wanted to fuck her.'

'How confusing, ' I said, lighting a cigarette.

'I wondered if it was because I'd been thinking about you before she exploded into my office,' Fleur said. 'Maybe. Anyway, I decided to protract the meeting, see her squirm a bit, and then I decided lunch. I knew Laurel and Hardy couldn't make it, so I took the bitch – Chris – over the road to The Compasses. They don't do a bad lunch there and she'd got me intrigued.'

'The bitch's name is Chris?'

'Chris Lawrence,' she said.

This was fun.

'What does she look like?' I asked.

'Rather good cheekbones,' Fleur said, 'Assisted blonde, no tits to speak of, good legs. You know, mini skirt and too old for it, but getting away with it. I had the feeling she gets away with rather a lot, and she sort of thawed a little over lunch. I'm making her do another projection, which is entirely unnecessary but I want to see her again. You don't mind, do you, Alex?'

I shrugged.

'None of my business,' I said. 'You're a free spirit, angel, and so am I. Sorry, that's a bit hippy, but it isn't – well – you and I are not talking marriage, Fleur.'

'I know,' she said, 'and, perverted slut that I am, I really want to go for it with her – and tell you all about it. But, if that's somehow not OK then I shall keep it to myself. If there is anything to keep. Am I making sense and, for god's sake, pour out some more wine.'

'Yes and yes,' I said, topping up her glass. 'Fleur, you never ask me about, well, my life, and I don't have the right to ask you about yours. If I want to tell you or you want to tell me, then fine, but I really don't feel we, well, owe it to each other. I like now and here with you. That's the way it is and it suits me.'

'Me too,' she said, 'and, Alex, I do wonder what else you do. And who. And how. But, as you say, 'tain't my business unless you want to make it that way. I wonder if it would be fun or tedious.'

Privately, I thought it would be quite a turn-on if I told Fleur I was fucking Chris Lawrence. But without being sure...

'Part of what I value about you, Alex,' she said, 'is your utter discretion. Being rather public in terms of work, it means I can relax with you entirely. There was a little liaison in the past which was fun – nothing like the fun we have, darling – and rumours got out that only she could have started. I am the Sphinx *à propos* my private life. One gets one's picture in the papers and one simply cannot afford a whiff of scandal.'

'Sweetie pie,' I said, for she looked like a serious little girl, 'have a chase of Chris Lawrence and I hope it's fun. If you want to give me a suck-and-fuck account of it all, then be my guest. If not, then don't. Just one thing, Fleur, and I won't say it again.'

'Serious?' she said.

'Serious,' I said. 'If it turns into In Love, then just tell me.'

'Of course,' she said immediately. 'You told me about that wretched Goddess of yours straight away. How is that going? I've been assuming no news is good news.'

'Pass,' I said. 'Well, she should be here this weekend. Don't spoil the evening. I'm handling it.'

'Remember I'm here,' she said. 'I have a feeling your weekend will be less pleasant than mine.'

'Oh?'

'Dinner with Chris on Saturday,' she said, catching my eye.

'That's my girl,' I said. 'Don't worry – I know you and 3 am phonecalls.'

'Well, there's the answerphone,' she said, 'and 7 am phonecalls with you are rather good news.'

I smiled. My voice on Fleur's answerphone while Chris was there? I thought not.

'And will you wear your linen suit on Saturday?' I asked her.

She threw back her head and laughed. 'Well, it does seem to be lucky.'

Our eyes danced, remembering.

Fleur had been late back once when I came over and still dressed for work. This suit was cream linen, and she wore it with black stockings and heels so high she walked like a circus pony. Which made the curves of her ass bounce neatly when she walked up the steps ahead of me. That, and the way her impossible heels stretched the black silk clinging to her calves, had me hotter than July by the time she put the key in the lock. I followed her, and threw her bag on the floor, ramming her up against the front door as she fought to hit the alarm buttons.

'Alex,' she had shouted, 'for fuck's sake, hang on.'

My shoulders and breasts pressed against her, and my hands raced down the rough fabric of her skirt. I thrust one hand under the hem, and felt myself gush with sheer desire as my fingers came in contact with the silk lining, then the smooth silk of her stockings, and the lace at the top, then her warm thighs. Fleur wore thongs and concentrated on her pelvic floor muscles and said she could have a lot of fun in meetings simply by crossing her legs. I felt the lace and satin V of her thong and my fingers slid between the cheeks of her ass, tugging the flimsy thing away from her flesh. Her nails dug into my jacket, then she tore it from my shoulders and threw her head back.

'Fuck me,' she said, eyes closed.

I slid one finger inside her, moving in deep circles and felt her open for me, wider and wider, and now three fingers pushed right into her as I heard her shoes fly across the hall and she slid down the door. Still I moved around, slowly and hard, the red hot wetness of her tugging me in, and she opened even wider, her muscles crushing my hand into a fist. I knelt in front of her and worked my fist gently into her, my other arm pinning her against the door. She spread both arms wide and stood shaking, as if she were on a crucifix. I looked up and all I could see was her neck and chin, head thrown back; all I could hear was her breathless moans.

'I want you,' she gasped. 'I fucking want you, fucking want you...' Over and over like a mantra. And I kneaded the inside of her, knowing that, if I touched the red and quivering clit inches from my face, she would come, and wanting only to keep on fucking her and fucking her and fucking her until she collapsed. And then I'd want to fuck her all over again.

I could smell the salty juice flowing over my fist, and it was the smell of a seashore and my mouth flowed with longing. The tip of my tongue hovered over her, and I breathed out hot breaths and watched her clit jump and flow, jerking and urgent. I stretched my tongue a little further and then my mouth was on her, clamped to her and sucking like a starving baby and we fell on the floor together, with her screaming and beating the boards with her fists.

But I wasn't done yet. I pulled her over so she lay face down, and pushed the crumpled skirt up over her ass. My hand was alive with the liquid smell of her, and I parted the cheeks of her ass and pushed a finger into her while she said *no, no, no* and arched against me. And now she was on all fours, grinding against me while my finger flew into the tight, demanding muscle like lightning. Suddenly she went limp and started laughing.

'You didn't even say hello,' she murmured, smiling and turning over to pull me to her. 'Sit on my face, Alex. This lazy girl needs to tongue-fuck you and I couldn't move for anything.'

And so I rode her mouth, thrilling at her tongue flicking against me, until a galaxy of stars exploded in my head and we lay together on the floor for a while, laughing and wrecked.

Now we were both giggling and she raised her eyebrows.

'You know that suit?' she said.

'I know that suit,' I said.

'Had to have it ultra-dry-cleaned,' she said. 'I went to a different dry cleaners, since, in this neighbourhood, I am considered a lady.'

'You? A lady? My, my, Fleur, you had me fooled.'

'Oh, I am a lady,' she said, reaching for a wok. 'Only when you're here I'm a slut, darling. And I love it.'

'I'll drink to that,' I said, wondering what on earth she had done to her attic.

Eighteen

We were eating from bowls glazed so deep their surface was liquid scarlet at the base with a rim of electric blue and turquoise metallic flake. I could feel the heat of the clay as she set the table. The two-pronged bronze forks had René Mackintosh twists to the handle, and there was a huge crystal salad bowl shaped like a leaf – or, as Fleur called it, the labia bowl. The aroma of fresh bread drifted over to me as she slid a basket onto the table.

She spooned prawns into our bowls, drizzling a vortex of sauce on and around them.

I put my hand on the small of her naked back and pulled her close, nudging her breasts with my mouth, and stroking the silky skin of her thighs.

'Eat,' she said, kissing my lips lightly.

I broke bread seeded with poppy and sesame, and did as I was told.

God alone knows what Fleur put in food, but it was always wonderful. She would grab tiny pots and jars and sniff each with a second's concentration, then toss a little in or put it straight back on the shelf. When she tasted her creation, she put a drop on the tip of her tongue and played with it – maybe for my benefit, but whatever, it was sexy as hell. Take these prawns – tiger prawns, of course – swimming in what looked like pale gold cream. The taste was green spice, then a burst of lime and tamarind and a curl of smoke adding a piquant tang. The texture was firm then flaky and scooped onto bread with the crunch of its hot crust, it was – as Fleur said – an oralgasm.

'Good?' she asked.

'Your foreplay always amazes me,' I said.

'It's very aphrodisiac,' she said, reaching for my hand.

I pushed my forefinger into her palm and felt an electric surge of sheer desire.

She let me play a while, then slid her hand away and served more food, her breasts pressed firmly into my shoulder. My finger curled into her navel, and her belly trembled under my palm.

Asparagus and adzuki beans, shiitake mushrooms, baby sweetcorn, lady's fingers, redcurrants, lychees and slivers of mango made a rainbow in the sunrise bowls. There was wild rice, too, laced with sesame and sunflower seeds and strands of samphire.

Fleur ate with her fork and hands, licking her fingers as her eyes laughed at me.

'Darling,' she said, 'have you ever sloshed?'

'I was watching that the other night,' I said, 'and I thought of you too.'

'It was the golden syrup,' she said. 'God, you know me and calories, but when that woman raised her arm and it made this fabulous sheer gold curtain – I think I could get into that.'

'I liked the chocolate spread,' I said. 'Mind, that was all tits and ass, right up my street.'

'I knew you'd like that,' she said, dangling mange tout so that it dripped onto her chin.

I leaned over and sucked her chin, drawing my face down to the exotic droplets on her breasts. She stroked some warm mango over my neck and ear and nibbled it away.

'Dear heart,' she whispered into my tingling ear, 'let's finish eating. I have an attic screaming for our appreciation but I am determined to feed us first. And, apparently, one needs a tarpaulin to slosh correctly. A tarpaulin very near a shower. I'll work on it.'

She sat back decisively then laughed, throwing her head back and her neck looked edible in the candlelight.

'Salad,' she said. 'You are atrocious with green vegetables, Alex. Let me vitaminise you.'

Green? This salad was every shade of green, with bruised purple and some leaves so white they looked silver, with chickpeas scattered like pearls, and viridian fronds of god knows what, fine as maidenhair and tasting of fire.

'And a sweet,' said Fleur, 'a nice messy one which you will consume with great delight.'

She whisked everything from the table, replacing it with two dishes heaped with what looked like snow. A sloosh of kirsch, a kiss of fire and soft flames of amethyst and aquamarine swam over the glistening surface, leaving a smooth café au lait skin. The tang of brandy, the savour of wild cherries – and Fleur's fingertips dabbling in fire. Under the sweet snow lay a heart of blood-red loganberries and spice.

'Perfect,' I told her.

'Slosh-worthy,' she said, her eyes sparkling.

One of her hands held mine as she led me up the curved stairs to the attic. In the other, she carried a silver bucket of ice and champagne. The last spiral of stairs was in darkness and, as we climbed, the air became warmer, thick with a perfumed garden of lilies, sandalwood, lavender, attar of roses.

'Close your eyes,' she breathed, and her hand tightened on mine. I heard the door creak and walked forward in blackness.

'Open,' she said.

Palm trees? Orchids? Lilies? The sound of water flowing and the sparkle of a fountain through the greenery and, as she led me deeper, it was a tropical glade, the floor artlessly covered with what looked like tiger skin, but my feet told me this was softer and thicker and warmer than the natural pelt of any wild animal. Fleur drifted to the floor and I went with her. She stretched and her shoulders arched like resting wings as she fiddled under a leaf, and white lights sparkled like stars overhead, in the trees, rolling back any awareness of walls or ceiling, and the sound of surf played in the air around us.

'Like it?' she asked.

'No,' I said, 'I love it.'

The lights cast shadows of lace across her smooth bare skin, and half-moons of deep shadow under her breasts. Between her thighs was midnight dark and her eyes glittered hypnotically. And now drums beat through the surf and she leaned towards me and kissed me with parted lips, stroking the tip of her tongue against my upper lip, then sucking my lower lip into her mouth. I drew my hand to cup her breasts, then slid down the silky sheen of her side, pushing my palm over her hip, kneading my fingers into the warm curve of her ass, hard down her thighs and calves, and I held her foot, drawing her leg up over me, fingertips beating softly against the soft dip where her inner thigh became fiery with heat and hair soaking with the inner juice of her.

She pushed my shoulders back fiercely and lay on top of me.

'My fantasy first,' she said, and talked into my neck while I kissed her ears, feeling the strong arch of her spine and her hips nudging against me. I listened to every wonderful word and clung to her shoulders.

And the game began.

I crept behind the tree and watched her, sitting on the rug, leaning back on her palms with her head lying back, eyes closed. Her flesh glistened with sweat and she poured champagne, tossing her hair away from her face, grazing her glorious neck with the base of the glass. I padded towards her and knelt behind her silently. She sipped champagne and I slid one arm around under her arm and kneaded her breast. She shuddered and melted against me. I took champagne into my mouth from the tilted crystal and fed it into her mouth as her hand raked my hair.

'Shall we walk?' I said, drawing her to her feet. And we did, around through the trees, until I held her against the trunk of one and we kissed deeply. Then I had to have her; my god, I wanted her and my hand dived to her belly, and she clamped her thighs together and said *no, no, no.* I held her hand and slid it up the bark, kissing her mouth hard and deep, and deeper and harder while I slid the leather band around the tree onto her wrist and she fought me. Hard and for real, that's what she wanted us to play, so I dragged her other arm to the next tree and tethered her there.

Still her thighs were clamped together, and she kicked out as I slid down her body and grabbed one ankle, forcing it against the next leather tie.

'Don't fucking tease me, bitch,' I growled at her, tearing at her other ankle, twisted around her other knee.

'No,' she said, 'no, don't, don't, I don't want this, you bastard.'

'But you do,' I told her, using all my strength to free her ankle, only to tie it with strips of dark leather, then standing back and looking her right in the eye.

She said again *no, no, no*, and I stepped back. She was totally in my power, just like she'd wanted in that throaty whisper as we lay on the floor.

I drank from her glass then refilled it and drank more. Her skin radiated heat as I put the icy neck of the bottle to her throat and lit a cigarette. then stepped back and let my eyes drink in every part of her taut and pinioned body.

I disappeared into the shadows as she moaned *what are you going to do to me, oh god, what are you going to do?* Her body was trembling as I crept up behind her and dribbled a little champagne down her spine and she struggled and twisted.

'You can see too much,' I told her, and slid a blindfold over her eyes. I ran my hand over her inner thigh and she thrashed away from my touch.

'And I want you to be still,' I said, finding the broad strip of leather at the base of the tree and caressing the small of her back with its rough surface. I slid both hands round her waist and crossed the rein, knotted it, and tied the free ends first to one tree then the other.

A spotlight picked out the twin curves of her ass and I knelt down, licking each cheek. I parted them then, and let my tongue run around her asshole, clenched tight and jerking, a perfect, tiny circled of soft pink, wrinkled like silk. The tip of my tongue pushed into the centre and she tried to pull away. My hands grabbed her hips and pushed her ass onto my face and I dipped into the jar of grease and massaged it into the cleft, and round and round until that gorgeous, tight-petalled asshole was shiny and flowing. I dipped my finger again into grease and worked the finger tip inside her. The muscle tore into me and I stood for a moment and let my teeth slide up her neck.

'I'm going to fuck you till you fucking scream for more, bitch,' I told her, then dropped to my knees again, and slowly slid my finger all the way inside her. Very gently and slowly I pulled my finger out of her, to the tip, then slid inside her, then out, then back into the heat of her. My other hand worked grease around two fingers and when I felt her ass loosen a little, I drew out the first finger and slid in two, again, slow, so slow, until I was sure of the tug and push of her. Then three fingers filled her and I worked up a rhythm. God, it felt amazing, and I stood behind her now, one hand clasping the crude knot at her waist, the other sure and fast in her, my hips bruising into her ass.

Then I stopped and she shook all over.

'You want more, bitch?' I said to her.

'I – no – no,' she said.

I shoved my fingers even deeper as she resisted.

'You want some more?' I demanded.

'Oh, god, yes,' she said.

'Then fucking beg for it,' I said, keeping perfectly still. 'Say it.'

'Just do it,' she said, 'do it, just do it.'

'Beg for it, say it, scream for it,' I told her, refusing to move a muscle although her body was dragging at my hand.

'I want it,' she said, 'I want it, oh god, I want it, please, god...'

'Say it, ' I said.

'Fuck me,' she said, gasping. 'I want you to fuck my ass.'

'How bad do you want it?' I said, keeping my voice cold.

'Very bad,' she said. 'I want you to fuck me...'

'Not good enough,' I said. 'Try again.'

'Fuck me, darling,' she said, *'fuck me till I scream.'*

That was the trigger and now my arm held her tenderly while my fingers flew round and back and forward and up and every way until a high-pitched sound started at the back of her throat, getting louder until a scream roared from her mouth like a train tearing out of a tunnel and she sagged against me, limp in all her soft shackles, and we were enmeshed, sweat pouring between us, her head lolling on my shoulder as I tossed her blindfold to the floor and kissed her closed eyes, rubbed my lips against her mouth and felt our mutual pleasure fizz in every cell of our bodies.

I loosened first one wrist then the other and she flopped unresisting into my arms. Once she was free, we lay motionless on the rug, clasped in each others arms. I felt her go even softer, and knew she was sleeping. Fleur – like a lot of people, I guess – looked like an innocent when she slept. All the studied movements of her face were at rest, the clever twinkle of her eyes was hidden, and the smile she had was sweet and slight, Sphinx-like. I love that feeling of total trust. She looked like a cat dozing on a sunny windowsill, one that flexes its claws a little, dreams of a midnight hunt playing in its mind.

I drew the blanket over us and slept for god knows how long, and Fleur was kissing me awake, leading me downstairs and into her bed, tucking a duvet round us both and putting a frothing glass against my sleepy lips.

'Call it breakfast, Alex darling,' she said, snuggling against me. 'The bloody birds have started already.'

We slept again, after dozens of soft, light kisses.

Nineteen

So, Friday I was purging my flat, needing to get around to Mrs Turner's plans, needing to shop for food for the Goddess, needing to run through any scenario she might choose to throw at me – Friday night? Saturday morning? Just when would our *whole weekend* start? I was damned if I'd ring her, though my sixth sense wanted me to. Maybe she wouldn't come at all, and I knew Fleur and Chris were going to be busy with each other.

Chris rang at eleven. 'Just feeling rather neglected,' she said, 'and randy as hell.'

'How nice of you to think of me,' I said, lighting a cigarette.

'Been busy with Mrs Turner?' she asked.

'Very,' I said, 'I'm going antique-hunting for her next week.'

'For her or with her?'

'For,' I said. For god's sake, Chris, lighten up!

'It's none of my business,' she said. 'Sorry.'

And who's got a sneaky date tomorrow, anyway, Chris? 'How was your heavy meeting?' I asked.

'Meeting?'

'Some heavy funding meeting with – oh, I don't know – some woman with an Irish name?'

'Oh, that,' she said. 'Just as I thought. She wants blood.'

I waited for more, but she wasn't giving any.

'Next week,' she said. 'You don't have to meet me, you know.'

'Chris,' I said, 'what's the matter?'

'Matter?'

'Yes, darling, matter,' I said. 'You seem determined to snap at me, and it is your phone call, so what is the matter?'

'Oh, bugger you, Alex,' she said. 'I rang really late last night and you were out. I feel like I'm just a number in your little black book.'

'If that *were* true,' I said, 'would it be so bad? Not that it is. *If* I had a little black book, it would be very selective and tiny.'

'I know about the Love of your life,' she said. 'That I can handle even if I think you're mad. I was just expecting you to – call me?'

'Hey, Chris,' I said, 'chill out. You said you were busy last night. That's your business. You want me to swing through the window clutching chocolates? Just tell me what you want and I'll see what I can do.'

'I don't know what I want,' she said, sounding cross and tearful.

'OK,' I said, taking a gamble, 'you want me to come over tomorrow night? You want to go to the pictures? Saturday night at the movies – back row? Huh?'

'I have arrangements for tomorrow,' she said quickly – *Chris, I know it!* – 'But what about Sunday?'

'I have arrangements too,' I said. 'Is there something wrong with Wednesday? Just tell me.'

'Wednesday's fine,' she said flatly. 'If it's Wednesday it must be Chris? You tell me.'

'It must be,' I said. 'That's what I'd like, anyway.'

'And what shall we do, Alex?' Now her voice was hard.

'Whatever you like,' I said, 'anything at all. I want to see you, Chris, I'm quite happy with whatever. If you want me to think of something, then I will.'

'I'm glad someone's happy,' she said.

This I did not need. And the conversation went on, her thrusting at me, me parrying, desperate to lighten her voice and bring in a little laughter and failing dismally.

'Wednesday, then,' she said, finally.

I let myself carry on hoovering over the sound of the phone

ringing five minutes later. The answerphone told me that it was Chris and she was sorry for being a prat, she just felt off today. That was true, but when she said it was nothing personal, I knew it was a lie. I hoped she'd calm down a bit, good god, she was gorgeous in bed, and a picture of her naked body filled my mind, the taste and smell of her filled my head. But if that phone call was a foretaste of what playing with Chris would cost, then she was going to be too much for me. I put it out of my mind 'till Wednesday.

But my mind kept on at me until I rang her home phone.

'Hey, sexy,' I said, 'whatever you're wearing, it's too much. I want to strip every thread from your body and eat you right now. You know who this is. And you know you want it too. See you Wednesday.'

That should pacify her.

I wanted to ring Fleur and talk dirty for a while, but there just wasn't time. Or so I thought.

The Goddess's first phone call came at five and she said she was just about to leave. Why the hell did I not believe her? Because I have a distressingly good memory.

I applied myself to Marjorie Turner's plans – at least I knew exactly what I was doing with her. I also applied myself to Jose Cuervo's tequila gold and health-giving orange juice, and wondered if it was sunrise or sunset with me and the Goddess.

When the second phonecall came at 8.30, my gut was swimming in enough cactus juice and vitamin C to set fire to Emiliano Zapata and his entire revolutionary army.

'You won't believe what's happened,' said the Goddess huskily.

'Well, try me,' I said, steeling myself for her next words.

'The bloody car won't start,' she said. 'I've tried everything and now the battery's flat.'

Surely she could have done better than that?

'I'm shattered, anyway,' I said, turning my sigh into a yawn, feeling tears at the back of my eyes.

'Oh, I am so disappointed,' she said, and if it had been the first time I'd heard it, I'd have been convinced.

'I'm calling the garage first thing in the morning,' she said.

She said a whole lot more, about love, talking, time, Marcie, karma, talking, bla bla bla.

After the words finished, after the silence of an ended call, and the BBC lady telling me to *please 'heng' up,* after the high-pitched howler ceased, I was still sitting there, clutching the receiver, paralysed. If I had been surprised, that would at least have been an emotion.

Like a robot, I called a taxi to take me to the nightclub. There at least lights would be flashing, semi-naked bodies dancing, people screaming and talking and touching, throwing themselves into a show of what passes for pleasure. And I could sit and watch them, and feel like I was alive.

Hell, I might even join the circus myself.

The Goddess turned up around midday, so why was my heart not skipping like a spring lamb? Instead, there was only a dull thudding, like a drum when the skin has gone slack. She let herself in, and I pretended I hadn't heard the key, the door, her footsteps on the stairs, the door opening – I concentrated on the finished and immaculate Turner drawings.

Then her lips brushed my neck, and my heart revved up as her arms wrapped round me. She held me strong and close, and a vibrato of breathtaking beauty ran through me.

'I need coffee,' she said, and I was half-way to the kitchen before my head grabbed the wild tattoo of my heart and screamed *be careful.* I put it down to the feelings of unease I'd had since the phone call from Chris. Thank god for the routine of water, plug, cup, coffee grounds; the war inside me had me dizzy with an instant headache, as if two less-than-friendly people were drilling into my temples for the hell of it. This was more than Chris.

Look right at her and be honest, my head said. Well, it would be a pleasure, my heart replied, trying to sound big and strong. My guts just whimpered, fearing the outcome, always the hapless victim of any emotional skirmish. I made myself a coffee too and won a battle about the breakfast lying scorned and useless in the fridge. Someone would eat it, if only the birds.

She was sitting smoking when I gave her the coffee and kissed her.

Look at her!

So I did.

Her thick blonde hair was pleated at the back of her head, and strands of it framed her face. Her eyes were a sombre grey and out of contact with mine, flicking here and there as the smoke rose from her lips. Well, no doubt there would be an hour or so of Marcie and then normal eye service would be resumed? Somehow I felt not, and lashed the fear down. Damn Chris!

Emilia hadn't taken her coat off, and why did I think of that as unusual? She liked to sit, this impossible and lovely woman, until she was baking hot, usually. Her fingers tapped lightly on her cup. Her long, corduroy-clad legs were crossed and her free foot was doing a tap dance in mid-air.

'Is the car OK?' I said, and her eyes jumped and confirmed that she had been lying – again.

'Fine,' she said, 'some bloody crossed wire.'

Madam, your Freudian slip's showing! I tried to ignore it. Tried also to ignore the acid reception my stomach gave to my first sip of coffee. Then...

'Alex, I can't stay,' she said, 'and there're things I need to say to you.'

My ears fizzed with a shock like electricity, numb as if slapped. So now give me the bad news.

'Well, that's OK,' my mouth said, 'things happen.'

'I mean, not now,' she said, 'and, well, not again. Never. It's not easy to say this, Alex.'

And I'm supposed to make it easy? I was struck dumb, only my hands alive, lighting a cigarette to give my frozen lips something to do.

'It's nothing to do with you.'

So have this conversation with someone else ...

'I've been doing a lot of thinking,' she said, and now it was my eyes that refused contact. 'I'm just not good at relationships,' she said hurriedly. 'The times I've just wanted to move in with you, Alex!'

Did I ask you? said my head, clutching at a strand of dignity.

'And you're lovely,' she said, 'but I'm no good for you.'

I developed an instant sympathy with the tumbrilled aristocracy of revolutionary France. My head tried to be clever, for I felt like I was drowning, like none of this was real, desperate to dive into a movie, to rewind to the moment her key had turned in the door, play it different – won't someone yell *cut!*

I found myself on my knees in front of her, my icy hands holding hers, my eyes searching for something in her eyes that simply wasn't there.

'You don't have to do this,' I said from another planet.

'But I do,' she said, and the ocean of her eyes was arctic. 'It's not fair on you and I should have said it a while ago.'

Like *when?*

'My life,' she said, exhaling fresh smoke, 'just doesn't seem to fit with a relationship. If it did, it would be you. But it doesn't. You've put up with all my crap for months and I'm grateful, but look at the time we have together, always rushed, always me.'

Suddenly my cheeks were running with water and my lips tasted salt.

'Real tears,' she said, brushing them away. 'I shouldn't be making you cry.'

'You've done it before,' I said, 'only you never saw them.'

'But I knew they were there,' she said, and the glaciers in her eyes melted as she pulled me into her breasts. 'I feel like such a bastard, Alex. I've known for ages it just wasn't going to work, and then you were so sweet and it didn't matter what I did or how awful I was, you just took it. It hasn't been easy.'

It was too much to feel her so close and hear what she was saying, so I pulled away and sat opposite her, trickling a little brandy into my coffee.

'Bit early for that, isn't it?' she said, holding her cup out. 'Me too, if you don't mind.'

'When have I ever minded anything to do with you?' I said.

'Never,' she said, 'and I'll always treasure everything about you.'

I looked at her.

I remembered lying on a beautiful bed in a hotel room with a balcony full of pink and white and purple geraniums. The room full of lilies, the sink full of ice cubes and peach champagne I'd had shipped in from Corsica. Me full to brimming with love. She wasn't there, of course. She would be four hours late. It was our first night-long date. We had never made love before. So I suppose I should have known from the start how it would be. I just never wanted to admit it.

Dinner with an angel and breakfast with the blues.

I wondered for a moment, as I made more coffee, if there was a second part to this *never*. Chastised myself for the straw-clutching, tried to come up with something real in this sudden nothing. Failed. Miserably.

And she sat there, silent now her cyanide capsule was delivered.

'So I guess.' I said, 'this is it.'

'Yes,' she said, 'I'm so sorry.'

'Just tell me one thing,' I said. 'I hate uncertainty. Two things.

One – when did you know it was over? And you've said never. Is that what you want?'

'I knew it was over,' she said, 'when I cancelled that last time I had a weekend and you were so sweet about it. I would have been angry.'

'I was furious,' I said, 'but what's the point? When you love someone...'

'...let them go,' she said, 'and if they are really yours, they'll come back. I've always said it, but never been able to do it. And you can and you do. It's frightening, being free like that, Alex. Not if you're on your own, but when you're with someone and they just – well, unconditional. And yes, I do want never. It hasn't been easy.'

Well, I just couldn't seem to find any words or sympathy for her, when, over the months, I'd done everything I could to sort out anything she'd found hard. Or maybe it was the fact that I couldn't find anything at all inside of me.

I suppose she left some time after that. I seem to remember her hoping I'd be all right, though god knows why. And something about it being the best thing and about me being able to get on with my own life. Part of me was running after her, smashing her car windows, biting the tyres, screaming *no*, but my legs didn't appear to be working.

It was about six before I moved. The phone had been ringing a few times somewhere in another galaxy. I stood and looked round the room, feeling I'd only just landed here and didn't know what anything was called, still less what it was for. There were papers with drawings on, two half-empty coffee cups, an ashtray half-full with stubs. This was my living room, I told myself, wishing myself a thousand miles and years away.

Something took charge, washed cups, packed papers and clothes. It then had me making a phone call to Tim, and leaving a message about Sunday not Monday. And god bless it, whatever it was, it then took me upstairs, drew the curtains and undressed me and put me to bed.

I slept like the dead, wishing I could be among them.

Twenty

I was driving through the dawn, heading south to Glastonbury to see Tim Smallboy about Marjorie Turner's piano. He'd faxed me photos of the disgraced rock star's effects – three grand pianos, a collection of enough gilt cherub lamps to furnish a Venetian brothel, a series of chaise longues and chairs in *fin de siècle* bordello scarlet plush, half a dozen life-size statues of young boys pouting like whores, and a marquee-size collection of sepia prints on the same theme. Tim said there were a lot more bits and pieces.

I remembered the strutting rock star in his heyday, *I l l l love you, baby, you're my sugar,* and so on. One for whom life had been financially lavish, syrup-sweet, enough to buy him turrets and high walls, a lake with swans, a degree of privacy so absolute that it had taken thirty years and the Internet to expose him. And all of his things auctioned just as if he were dead.

I had not told Marjorie the origin of the pianos, just their immaculate moneyed pedigree. She favoured the white one, but dithered about the yew, where the inlay looked marvellous, swirls of fine ivory and gold lines. She had left it to me to make the final decision, worrying that too much white would be clinical. I had a photo of the room in my case, and would do a mental montage once I had seen all Tim had to offer.

I like Glastonbury – the open-air lunatic asylum, as Tim called it. Old hippies with armchair communism still intact, and mortgages and children at private schools. Tim operated a few miles into the country, from an old vicarage he had built up from derelict to immaculate some ten years ago. There was a barn where he kept most of his ever-changing stock, and although he had a high street shop, most of his business was done from home, on a cash or goods basis. I had a Las Vegas gambler's wodge of George Turner's currency stashed in my car, and that had thrilled him, once the words *priceless* and *bargain* entered the equation. George liked to feel like a wheeler-dealer. Tim didn't know who I was buying for, otherwise his prices would double. I'd heard him on the phone too many times, forcing bids against imaginary buyers, to trust him an inch.

But for all that, I liked him. The two years I'd lived in Glastonbury, being married Jodie's bit on the side, he'd been a real lifeline, always ready with a sarky queeny quip, a bottle or three of foolproof amnesia, a microwave banquet and a bed for the night when it got too much in my empty love-nest. He'd even borne with my endless replays of *Visions of Johanna* tangling up my mind and heart until wine left me unconscious. The last few months of my time in Glastonbury I'd lived in the vicarage, licking my wounded heart into shape before I moved on. Tim had got me into resin, too, figurines and heads which he then doctored to antiquity. When I say resin, I don't know what else he put in it – a Smallboy speciality, this production of very exclusive antiques. They came out with the texture and weight of stone, or porcelain, or clay. He liked working with me, knowing I would say nothing to his clientèle about the attic workshop over the vicarage, and having me as a lodger added a little credence to his flimsy persona of a heterosexual widower.

I stopped at a Little Chef and filled up on coffee and gas and called him.

'We're having a dinner party, Alex,' he said, 'some of the old faces longing to see you. And are you alone? You're in the four-poster, anyway.'

'Unless I see something gorgeous thumbing a ride, I'm alone,' I said.

'That's unusual,' he said. 'Do I need to stock up on Kleenex?'

'No, Tim,' I said, 'this is a business trip. High-powered Alex Scott meets serious art collector and spends someone else's money. I can't be forever chasing skirt, dear.'

He laughed. 'Just get here,' he said, 'I need to see your face before I can believe a word you say. Young, free and single? We'll see.'

The words played in my head as I drove through the curving Somerset hills. Young? Well, old enough to know better and young enough to have fun. Free? I was free, so why did that make me sigh a little? I should have seen the Goddess/Groke coming and failed to be dazzled by the image. Single? Determinedly so – Fleur and I were having L-free fun, and Chris was trying an emotional number I was not prepared to sign on for. Which she knew. If I kept her away from late-night 70% proof blues, she was fine. But more and more, I had noticed how she was one of those drunks who goes suddenly into maudlin – *in vino* exaggeration, as an actress said to me years ago. I felt Chris was wanting some kind of commitment and thought enough sex would get me feeling that way too. Sex and a sudden preoccupation with make-up, the mention of a joint holiday, all the signs were there and if it had been don't-give-a-damn Fleur, then I'd be playing. Chris seemed to be wanting a man in her life, or me as a role-playing woman, and I don't do that. I mean, if I wanted a man, I'd get one. And if I wanted to be a man I'd get myself a good shrink. Can't stand that square-assed butch acting bit. Chris had a moodiness that I couldn't be bothered with; it was all about her three failed marriages and abandoned teenage children. As a friend I'd listen, but as a relationship? Uh oh. I had sworn off In Love and was damned if I'd break that 5 am promise to my sanity.

And there were those three phone numbers I'd collected in the club before the Goddess/Groke had blown me out. A dark, curly-headed teenager who'd tried to buy my drinks, a Goth with alarmingly long black nails, and a lady in a vest that sparkled like the Manhattan skyline as we danced, her tanned arms resting lightly on my shoulders, her shimmering lips laughing and leaving a crescent moon of lipstick on her glass. The trouble was, I couldn't remember whose number was which, and I really didn't want to call the Goth or the teenager.

'Alex, you look great,' Tim said, opening the door. 'The wine is cooling and all my cooking is done.'

'Piano,' I said, 'before you get me pissed, Tim. I mean it. Business first, sweet Smallboy, then pleasure.'

'OK,' he said. 'God, you get tougher every time I meet you. Let me get the keys.'

We walked through the orchard, trees heavy with purple plums, fallen fruit scenting the air in the drowsy Somerset midday. He pushed the barn door open and flicked on the lights.

'Jesus, is that a Bugatti?' I said.

'Our fallen idol collected cars,' he said lightly. 'A pink bloody Rolls and a Cadillac, a couple of tiger-skin Mercs, a Mustang – all very predictable, but I had to have this. It won at Monte Carlo before you or I were ever a twinkle in anyone's eye. Does your new and stinking client have an eye for cars?'

'Not that I know,' I said. 'I could work on it.'

'Oh, don't work too hard,' he said. 'I might keep it for a while. If only to sit in and have a swank.'

Tim's deceased lover Harold – his fictional wife Harriet – had loved classic cars, and after he died, Tim had got rid of the scarlet Rolls that had taken them all over England and Europe for so many years. He'd virtually given it away, then tried to buy it back but it had gone to Kuwait and he said maybe that was good, because if he'd ever seen it again he would have stolen it.

'Pianos,' he said with a flourish. 'Take your pick.'

He left me and went back to the Bugatti. Tim never applies pressure and if I decided on nothing at all, it wouldn't matter. I pulled my papers out of the case and sat for a while. The white

Bechstein or the yew Bluthner? The glossy black Steinway was out, too concert hall for Marjorie. I took a closer look at the inlay on the yew. It was an intricate pattern of stylised roses and apples, the grain perfect, slivers of gold and ivory highlighting the curve of the petals and apples. I could almost feel the craftsman placing it all, and the hundreds of paid hands that had polished the liquid surface for decades. And a white piano is a white piano is a cocktail lounge or an album cover.

When I stood back a little, I nodded. In the scrolls below the apples, if you were just a little imaginative, you could pick out the letter T. As in Turner.

I rang Marjorie and told her dodgy butler whom he might say was calling to Madam.

'Alex?' she said. 'How's it going?

'I'm standing beside your piano,' I told her, 'It's light gold, Marjorie, and the strangest thing – it has the initial T in the inlay. Two "t"s, actually, intertwined.'

'Oh?' she said brightly ,'that's marvellous, Alex. What about the white?'

'No,' I said, 'Too white. It would detract from your sofas. You were right, you know, too clinical. The yew is – well, *you,* if you know what I mean. I can almost see you playing it. And it's a Bluthner.'

'Ye-es,' she said, 'You know what George is about buying British, Alex.'

'I think even George would appreciate this,' I said, paying lip service to his supposed cultural superiority. 'This is unique. I'll tell you what. I'll haggle with the man here when he comes back. I think he's not quite aware of what he's got here, so I'll do my utmost for you.'

'I don't know what I'd do without you,' she said. 'Ring me back and let me know. Or shall I ring you? This *is* the expensive time of day.'

I loved Marjorie's ideas of economy.

'I'll call you,' I said.

I walked over to where Tim was lounging in the Bugatti.

'Let's do business,' I said.

Twenty-one

Tim was singing as we walked back through the orchard, as any man might be who had just trousered £33,000. I was smiling too, with £7000 to spare. Change of £3000 for dear George and Marjorie, and four for me – a fair commission, I thought. Tim had started at fifty, ten more than I would go, and our haggling had been brief and cosmetic.

We sat out in the garden with a bottle of Chablis and a dish of fiery Japanese rice crackers.

'This the life,' Tim said. 'Well, it's what passes for life, anyway. And how are you? I don't want to pry, as one is supposed to say, but when you're not getting any, it's the next best thing. Give me the dirt.'

I laughed and told him about the Goddess/Groke, and he tutted. 'Should never stay where the *grand amour* treats you less well than a friend,' he said.

I told him about Chris, and he groaned. 'Heartbreak Motel on the horizon – if not for you, then for her and you being you you'll start mopping it up. Lose it, Alex.'

Then I told him about Fleur – well, some of it.

'Verily, thou hast saved the best till last,' he said mockingly. 'Do I detect a hint of In love there?'

'That's what's odd,' I said. 'No. That was a ground rule when it started and, do you know, I think we might be sticking to it. Which is unusual. Maybe I've just met a slag like me for once.'

'No, no,' he said. 'The thing is, you're both playing and you carry on playing. Your Fleur is never going to accuse you of failing to buy milk and I believe that – pathetic though it sounds – is the root cause of many a dismal break-up.'

I told him how she was making moves on Chris and he choked on his wine.

'*Too* priceless,' he said. 'Chris must be rather attractive? I thought so. What about a threesome, do you think?'

'Don't like them,' I said. 'Only done it once and it didn't feel good.'

'Don't you like to watch?' he asked, 'or is that a man thing? Maybe it's my age, but I have a couple of rather decorative young men who come in and *do* for me – not often, I have to say, but I really rather enjoy it. What about that?'

'Not my scene, Tim,' I said, 'I'm a player.'

'Well, you need to be in love,' he said firmly. 'Tragedy gives you an edge, Alex, and in god knows how many years I've never known you *happy* In Love, but never quite alive either unless you are in love.'

'Fair comment,' I said, 'but I'm really trying to wean myself off it this time. I guess my Ms Right got run over by a bus years ago.'

'You know, he said, 'I think you love In Love because it's totally out of your control. Look at your life, dear. You earn nice money, drive a rather snazzy car, live in a rather bijou *pied à terre* – you've taken control since that bloody woman you hung out with here – what was her name?'

'Jodie,' I said, rinsing the syllables from my mouth with a gulp of wine.

'Yes,' he said, 'the lovely Joanna. Wrist-slitting time – and for what? The fizz in the loins? The sparkle in the eye? The monsoon of juices flooding your body?'

'All of that,' I said, 'and the dreams and the visions, Tim. I'm rather lost without a dream.'

'So, what's your dream, Alex?' he said softly, serious for a moment.

'My dear Smallboy, I don't think I have one right now 'and

that's a bit of a panicky feeling for me. Oh, I have bits of dreams, you know, and Fleur plays seriously amazing games, and that's fab, but my dream is like a scattered jigsaw. with pieces missing. Well, one piece. I need to have She, The One, and the dream builds around her. No She, no dream.'

'My dream died with Harold,' Tim said, 'but at least I have memories. Years of them.'

'That's rather what I'm lacking,' I said. 'Memories, yes, but all brief and then come the memories of endings and I really hate that bit. Jesus, I have sacrificed religiously at the altar of love, and it seems the gods are smirking at me   try again, Alex! You know, when it's late night alone, I almost ring the bloody Goddess. I won't but I had to talk to myself very seriously the other night.'

'All grown up and never learnt how to crawl, my pet?' said Tim.

'Open another bottle,' I said. 'Let's change the conversation, Tim, it's getting too close.'

I had a moment or so alone, and let the sun blaze on to my closed eyes until Tim came back with Pouilly Fumé.

'So who's coming tonight?' I asked him.

I was a little uneasy when he said he couldn't quite remember, then fed me a couple of vaguely familiar names. Tim is a shit actor, and I just had the feeling he had something up his expensively cuffed sleeve.

Twenty-two

When Tim did dinner, it was always an occasion. His galleried hall lent itself to theatre, and he had all the props to create the splendour of Hollywood, or Grand Opera. When I first knew him, he had a cat called Tosca because she had a habit of throwing herself from the gallery with a blood-curdling screech.

Tonight, the backdrop was *Sunset Boulevard – the movie, darling, not the Lloyd Webber* – and Tim and I arranged half a dozen life-size musicians from the Thirties at one end of the room. He dragged a potted palm and two huge and sombre aspidistras among them to complete the effect. My job was music and arranging the speakers so that the plaster figures would seem to be playing for real.

'Shame you don't do swishy long dresses, Alex,' he said. 'That staircase is crying out for Norma to make an entrance. And my drag days are rather distant. Might upset the guests.'

'Who's coming?' I asked, but he remained elusive, his watch bidding him to the kitchen, while he banished me to the bathroom. No point in arguing when he was in this bossy mood, so I lounged around in a sunken bath made for at least three, letting the jets beat the weariness from my body.

In my room, I dithered. *Sunset Boulevard*? I couldn't be Norma Desmond, and neither did I wish to be Jo Gillis. I hadn't the figure to be von Stroheim, either. Maybe I was the poor dead monkey. I settled for a sort of Byronesque look with Zoë Wanamaker mad hair, a white silk shirt which was all sleeves and skin-tight black velvet pants and boots. I had to admit I looked good and Tim nodded approval.

'Very Hamlet,' he said. 'You're much better androgynous, Alex, keep them guessing.'

'But darling,' I said, 'I am all woman.'

'You have the rampant appetite of a queen,' he said, 'and the grace of a hummingbird which then mutates into a tigress closing in for the kill. Don't forget, Alex, I've seen you through many incarnations. That poor weepy little thing that I adopted twenty years ago, my god! She was such a sad little girl, *she* turned my hair grey! And, baby, just look at you now! That's better – there is a timber wolf lurking in your smile, my dear...and where did she come from?'

'The appalling Zee,' I said.

'Yes,' he said, 'she gave you an edge. And the cream-filled pussy – pardon my intended vulgarity – I assume she comes from Fleur?'

'Probably,' I said, thinking of Fleur's post-orgasmic purrs.

'But always the alley cat,' he said. 'That Chris has kept that there – passion, yowling at the moon and so much of the moment – knowing the next day's moon brings another *grand amour*!'

'Oh, Tim,' I said, 'moi?'

I looked him in the eye. It was, after all, Tim who taught me the chameleon technique of survival.

'Alex, I award you a daily Oscar,' he said.

'You have something atrocious planned for this evening,' I told him, 'I'd like to see the script.'

'Script? Alex! Life is improvisation. All I can do is set the scene and invite the cast.'

Who turned out to be seven – Tim's lucky number being nine.

First came Steven and Josh, the two young men who 'did' for him – tall, muscled, preening and decorative, winning the daily battle with the horror of ageing, The soft light made them an eternal mid-twenties, and *don't they look marvellous, you'd never know they clock up 81 years between them,* Tim murmured to me.

Then Cilla and Bill, where the connection was antiques. Bill did big fairs and Cilla bred show dogs. I heard them arguing before they knocked at the door, something about his sense of direction and her inability to park. When they came in they were smiling at the rest of us, then sat far apart, his eyes hard and hurt, hers flashing as her loud and educated voice swirled around Tim.

When the next knock came, I was in the kitchen, drowning gin for Cilla, and icing mineral water for Bill. I gave them their drinks before I saw the next guest, and cursed Tim, thanking whatever gods stand up for bastards that I can act.

She was standing there, all Mother Earth – patchwork Khatmandu skirt in purples and reds, a fawn velvet top embroidered in the same colour across her fabulous breasts, chunky necklaces and a rope of auburn hair glinting in a plait in the candlelight. He'd really surpassed himself this time, bloody Tim – no wonder he'd been vague about the guest list.

Jodie.

Tim at least had the grace to be talking to her while I searched for a way to greet her.

She was, after all, the only reason I'd met Tim in the first place. And it was a good many years ago. But it had hurt so much at the time that I'd never said goodbye to her, just left for San Francisco, courtesy of a Smallboy subsidy and contacts that led to my courier years. All those evenings of crying together in her car, wonderful afternoons exploring her naked body, nights of knowing she was lying beside – beneath – on top of – her bloody husband, who, to cap it all, really liked me and treated me as a good mate.

I decided to talk to Steven and Josh, who were examining our orchestra.

'Tim's said a lot about you, Alex,' said Steven, his brown eyes twinkling in unlikely eyelashes.

'Ditto, darlings,' I said, 'and I'm sure it was all true.'

'He's so clever,' said Josh, with his grown-up cherub lips.

'You can say that again,' I said.

'Oh,' Steven said, 'What's he been doing now?'

I toyed with the idea of telling them about Jodie, then decided no. I hadn't seen her for all these years, and most of them I hadn't even thought about her. 'Selling me a piano,' I said. 'You boys might be able to inspire me, actually.'

I moved on to the safe ground of the Turners and their mansion and soon they were hooked on the Elvis swimming pool, Josh offering himself as groundsman, Steven telling me how good he would be as a houseboy – he and Marjorie could do needlepoint together.

Tim came towards me, his eyes twinkling. 'I must have you circulate, Alex,' he said. 'We all know each other on a regular basis, you are my star guest.'

'Twinkle, twinkle,' I said, strolling with him. 'If there is a tea tray in the sky, may it crash onto your head, Tim. When did you decide to have this haunting?'

'You're not cross?' he asked. 'Surely enough time has gone by – and I do work with her.'

'Just remind me how many Oscars I have,' I said. 'I don't like surprises like this.'

It was strange to come face to face with Jodie. That face I'd sketched, dreamed of, kissed – loved. Those lips that had sucked me to dizzying orgasm, those eyes that had laughed and wept when there was nothing between us but sweat. And here she was, her fingers round the stem of a wineglass, fingers that had explored me so gently, then with a passion that had me delirious.

'Well, hi, Jodie,' I said, remembering her breast on my lips – it was Jodie who had wakened in me my total devotion to the curve and heat and weight of the female breast, the magical softness of a nipple, the rapturous hardening on my tongue.

'Alex,' she said, 'this is a surprise. I don't think I would have recognised you.'

I smiled as I recalled her holding my face the very last time we'd been lovers. *Learning me by heart,* she'd said.

'One changes,' I said.

She half-smiled.

'Your eyes never change,' she said.

I think we were supposed to exchange knowing glances – Jodie had always had a way of looking into my eyes that made me feel she touched my soul. Damned if I would!

'Windows of the soul?' I mocked her lightly.

'Your soul never changes,' she said, a little lower.

'Not sure about that, Jodie,' I said, 'define soul.'

But as she started to speak, there was the sound of breaking glass and Cilla swore.

'Damn you, Bill, I won't have you tell that story! If anyone is going to tell it, I will and I bloody well won't!'

Tim whisked the shattered crystal from around Bill's feet, and Steven and Josh stepped back.

'You have a point, dear,' Bill said, icily polite.

'I think it's a domestic,' Tim said. 'Let me freshen your drink Cilla, come and tell me what you'd like. I don't think I have arsenic, my sweet.'

She followed him into the kitchen and soon there was staccato laughter between her pithy character assassinations of Bill.

'Oh, god,' Jodie said, 'she's off.'

'Friend of yours?' I said.

'Glastonbury is very small,' she said. 'Everybody knows everybody face to face or by reputation, and Cilla does this rather a lot.'

'It's been a long time,' I said, remembering the cosy hippy kitchen atmosphere.

'We've all grown up,' she said. 'Well, I suppose that's the point. Not grown up, just grown older, Alex. We all live too close not to know each other's little foibles, and after a while, everyone's rather predictable. You just know Cilla will be shouting and throwing things at Bill, then it all calms down – he does a sort of adoring repentant swain and she becomes centre-stage queen and then we're all allowed to have a nice evening. Tim didn't tell me you'd be here.'

'Ditto,' I said. 'Would you have come?'

'Would you?' Now our eyes met.

'Yes,' she said, 'if only to find out what happened to you. You just vanished, Alex, and Tim wouldn't say where. Or why.'

'Surely you sussed out why?' I said, rather enjoying the low intimate tone of her voice, and – Jesus! – she was still wearing the same perfume. Vetiver.

'Alex, I was totally confused,' she said. 'One evening we were together, like we always were on Thursdays – remember? Then it was Monday and you didn't come, and no one knew where you were. Tim had gone to France and I was frantic until he came back. He said he didn't know where you were. I didn't know what to think.'

I smiled and sipped my drink. I had forgotten the way things were with us, but yes, we had been Thursday and Monday evenings – Martin's nights for chess and circuit training. And then there were always Wednesday afternoons – Jodie's half days, which often ended with me eating *en famille*.

'Well, we weren't exactly going anywhere from what I remember, darling,' I said, 'so I thought one us had better – go somewhere, I mean. So I went. The doorbell, Jodie, I'd better be hostess since Tim is still in the kitchen with Cilla.'

I opened the door, wondering if this would be another blast from the past, still wondering how to play things with Jodie, what had happened to Martin, and how much anyone apart from Tim knew about our shared history.

'I'm Alex,' I said to the couple on the step, 'a house guest. Tim's in the kitchen. Do come in. Let me introduce you to everyone – get you a drink?'

'Paul,' said the bearded man, taking my unoffered hand.

'Jane,' the woman said, smiling at me, 'and we know the others, but a drink would be lovely.'

'Brought some home-made,' Paul said, pulling two bottles from the sagging pockets of his parka, 'Organic, no hangovers. Tim says they're good. One elderberry and sloe, one damson and blackberry. Mine's a beer.'

'Tim knows what I like,' Jane said, twisting her dark hair up on the back of her head. As I headed for the kitchen, I heard her greeting Jodie with air kisses and *darling!*

Cilla was waving one arm around, the other entwined round Tim's shoulders as she wept.

'Alex,' Tim said, 'Cilla is fine.'

'Sure,' I said, 'Paul and Jane are here, mine host, and apparently you know what Jane likes to drink.'

'Oh, I'll put him down,' said Cilla, 'Smallboy, you are my fantasy lover and an angel and I'm bloody well going to make Bill jealous, the bastard. Sorry, Alex, do you think I'm awful?'

I looked at her hair, sprayed into fake blonde and careful disarray, her immaculate tan sheen, the slightly smudged apricot lips, mirrored in manicured nails. Her sweater was pink and orange House of Fraser stripes, and her knee-length skirt picked up the pink to perfection. She had the sort of hiking, biking Head Girl legs that had probably magnetised Bill however many years ago. And her mascaraed lashes fluttered around eyes as blue and hard as Wedgwood.

'Awful, Cilla?' I said, and laughed, 'I think you're rather marvellous. A great actress.'

'God, you are perceptive. Isn't she perceptive, Tim? Nobody knows how much I act, Alex, nobody. Especially Bill. He's a cold fish, Alex. Never marry a cold fish.'

I took a beer from the fridge for Paul and told her I never would.

'I like you, Alex,' she told me, with practised spontaneity, swaying towards me.

'God, no!' Tim shrieked and she stopped.

'Don't give Paul a cold beer,' Tim said, 'I have real ale for him otherwise we get a lecture. And is that his wine? How very kind. Cilla, would you give Paul his beer, my angel?'

He ushered her back into the hall then came back his shoulders shaking.

'Such an old tart, dear,' he said. 'She really is a monster, Alex, wasted on us all. I think of Joan Crawford. Don't tell me you were going to flirt with her! Too, too priceless!'

'Watch me go,' I said. 'Tim – why Jodie, for chrissake?'

'You're the one who left us all,' he said. 'Consider this penance. Your sins will find you out. You should talk to her, Alex. I had years of why-why-why with young Jodie.'

'Simple,' I said, 'Martin. End of story.'

Tim looked at me as he mixed Jane's drink.

'What happened to Martin?' I said.

'She threw him out,' he said, 'Five years after you, the cracks were too wide to paper over and she found he had a bit on the side. Sauce for the goose, darling, but she couldn't bear the taste of it on the gander. If you had stuck around, Alex, all heaven would have been yours. She's never settled with any one since.'

'Oh, crappy and tardy matchmaker,' I said, 'give me one of whatever Jane's having, darling. I need five to get my bearings.'

Twenty-three

Jane's drink had a slightly less-than-pleasant metallic undertone – Tim said it was coconut – but it hit the spot. I knew this man and his tongue-loosening cocktails – he would slide between all of us, topping up glasses to heighten emotions and create dramas for as long as possible, and only then would we eat. I drank half of the glass he had given me, then washed the taste away with icy water, deciding to stick to wine for the next little while.

'This is my saviour!' Cilla shouted as I rejoined the party, 'someone who knew *me* straight away! That is so rare – Alex, come and sit next to me!'

'Lovely,' I said, treating her to a smile.

Her muscled thigh snuggled into me, and one hand clung to my shoulder – I guess for Bill's benefit. She had Josh perched on the arm of the sofa on her other side, and her fingertips drummed his knee. Let the boy look embarrassed; I decided to enjoy the pantomime.

'Such an interesting shade,' I said. 'Orange.'

'Do you think so?' she shrieked, and the gin fumes burned my face.

'Not everyone can carry it,' I told her, catching Josh's eye as he giggled into his glass.

'Cilla can wear anything.' Bill said, 'or nothing. Always looks marvellous.'

'Bill!' she howled, flinging herself painfully against me, her nails digging into my arm.

'I think we should dance,' he said.

'Bill, I don't want to dance,' she said, but she let him pull her to her feet, and clasp her in an expert and familiar way and whirl her away from the sofa. Let the burlesque begin!

Josh slid into her seat. 'I thought she was after me,' he whispered.

'She was, my love,' I said, 'and me, and the entire orchestra, whatever and whoever it would take to bring Bill to heel.'

'Just suppose,' Steven said, dropping to the other side of me, 'I mean, I don't know, but would you have, you know – done it with *her*, Alex?'

I watched the couple whirling around the room. She should have been wearing yards of tulle and sequins, he should have been monkey-suited.

'Bit athletic and noisy,' I said. 'She'd demand conversation – probably shout out instructions, do you think? Rather fête-opening, scout-mistressy, not altogether my type.'

And now Tim joined us. The cabaret had started and we were in the queer corner.

'We're just being filthy old queens asking Alex if she'd have a go at Cilla,' Steven said.

'Big knickers and an upholstered brassière?' Tim said.

'Don't you believe it,' I said, 'Cilla is the girly-wirly undies type. Probably black or scarlet to keep the old man in some sort of erotic fantasy. Satin and lace. Suspenders. A basque.'

'Bet you,' Tim said.

'A hundred,' I said, 'only, if I have to find out all by my shy little self, I want danger money.'

'You're on, Ms Scott,' said Tim, 'and I doubt there'll be a need for danger money.'

By now, Bill and Cilla had their hands up each other's shirt and jumper, but however we craned and peered we couldn't find an answer to our bet.

'Give it a little time,' Tim said, 'and give me your glasses.'

Jodie came over, dodging Bill and Cilla and what had turned into a rather good tango.

'Come to join the boys?' said Steven. 'Our Jodie is an enigma, Alex. You sussed Cilla, what about Jodie?'

I smiled up at her, let my eyes flicker over to Jane and then back.

'A lady with secrets,' I said, 'and a perfect right to keep them.'

'Swap me a secret, Jodie,' Steven said.

She managed a laugh.

'Is that the best you can do, Alex?' she asked. 'Everyone has secrets.'

'She's in love,' Steven said dramatically. 'Are you, Jodie?'

'Oh, Steven, everyone's in love,' she said.

'I bet Alex isn't,' he said. 'Are you? Have you ever been?'

'Oh yes,' I said, 'very much so. Good god, Steven, I invented it.'

'And did she break your heart?'

'Into a million pieces,' I said, 'like the mirror in *The Snow Queen*, Steven.'

'*The Snow Queen*?' he said, 'Who's in that? Or is it someone we know?'

'Hans Andersen,' Jodie said. 'It's a fairy tale. With a happy ending, of course.'

'It's a book, not a film,' said Josh. 'Wasn't he Swedish?'

'Danish,' I said. 'Scandinavians have a way of capturing heartbreak and true love all at the same time. Think of Garbo – or Viveca Nielsen.'

So Jodie knew that I remembered her Danish grandmother and the way she claimed her cheekbones were almost pure Viking. I smiled and stood up, offering her my seat. As she sat, I moved over to Paul and Jane, saying something about drinks. I didn't miss the slightly stung look in Jodie's eyes, just chose to ignore it for the time being.

I avoided Cilla's octopus arms and strolled to where Jane and Paul were sitting. 'Lurchers,' Jane was saying as I joined them,

'God, look at them! Such energy.'

'Cilla breeds them,' Paul said, seeing me look puzzled. He nodded to where Cilla and Bill were hoofing it up and I smiled.

'Lanky, vicious, persistent things,' Jane said.

'And dogs are like their owners,' Paul said, sighing. 'I know, darling. Jane doesn't like dogs being bred – Alex, isn't it?'

'Not when there are sanctuaries and pounds full of strays and abandoned dogs,' Jane said. 'What do you think?'

'I like dogs,' I said. 'My lifestyle doesn't quite fit with one, or two – or even three – no, three is a pack. But I have a plan to adopt from one of those rescue places when I grow up.'

'We did,' Jane said, 'and bloody Cilla said it – IT, I ask you – she's a she, should have been put down. As if I'd even asked her.'

'What sort?' I said.

'Mainly terrier – Heinz 57, but a bit of collie so the legs look strange. Very destructive and then she looks shocked at the bloody devastation. She's not so bad now.'

'Now everything is made of metal,' Paul said. 'Used to be all wood. A bit modern for us. Let me get you a drink.'

I liked his attitude.

'I gather it's been a long time since you were here,' Jane said, as soon as he went.

'Yeah,' I realised from the look she gave me that Jane knew about me and Jodie. 'Years,' I said, meeting her eyes.

'I know,' she said, 'Maybe I should shut up, but I think you need to talk to her.'

'Do you? Do I?' I said, glancing to where Jodie was sitting laughing with the boys.

'I met Jodie when she split with Martin,' Jane said, 'It must be wonderful to just vanish, Alex – was it?'

'It's just something that seems to happen,' I said, 'and – well, it was a long time ago.'

'I'll shut up,' Jane said. 'You're rather different from how I imagined. But talk to her, Alex. How long are you here?'

'Don't know,' I said. 'Got to arrange transport for a piano and some other bits of Tim's. A couple of days?'

'Good,' said Jane. 'You talked about when you grow up – well, find some time alone with Jodie.'

Hey, lady, butt out! Before I could switch the conversation or move, Tim rang the gong and I wondered who would be sitting next to me. As I passed him, I murmured *not Jane,* and he nodded.

'Don't worry, my pet,' he said.

He had a huge circular dining table with place names and I wound up between Cilla and Josh. Steven was on Josh's other side next to Tim, and hostile Jane was to his right. Then Jodie, Paul and Bill beside his flushed and laughing wife whose pink thighs splayed towards him. And then me. Cilla was lurching, all right.

I was facing Jodie and I smiled at her under the score of candles burning in Tim's chandelier. Mirror balls at each corner of the room caught the light and swam dreamy, pale-gold circles on the lilac walls and ceiling. Jane noticed the smile and I could feel her trying to make eye contact with me. Well, tough, I was busy working out the dynamic Tim had planned – he sat like a spider in a web.

I wondered who else knew about the ancient history of me and Jodie. Probably Paul – Jane was the best-friend-as-husband type. Cilla and Bill were far too absorbed in their own psychodrama to notice anything that didn't affect them. Steven and Josh probably knew – Mr Smallboy was the world's worst gossip. I had a sudden feeling that I might just be the floorshow and any appetite I had vanished.

I wanted a cigarette more than anything. So I lit one.

But the small talk spiralled around and Cilla was so loud I relaxed and took the time to watch Jodie.

Jodie without Martin – just what I had dreamed and hoped and prayed for. *Twenty years ago!*

And we ate – and Josh started talking quietly to me. About

Steven and how wonderful he was and how his life had been meaningless until they met. I became aware of Cilla's thigh pressing against mine and ignored it. She was flushed with gin and decrying Bill's sense of adventure, and asking if anyone ever *really* used a vibrator. I thought of the Big Fun Boy and the Piccolo Playmate and Chris's cute blonde ass – and Josh murmured *how embarrassing*. So I told him I used dozens and he sniggered and said they did too.

All the time I was aware of Jodie. Age had only made her lovelier and I wondered why Jane was so insistent on me talking to her *à deux*. She could not – surely to god? – still be carrying a torch for me? Did she want to hit me? Accuse me of abandoning her? I knew with a familiar lurch that I still fancied the pants off her and what the hell did that mean to me now?

Another cigarette.

'What have you been up to?' Jodie said, just as I was about to ask her the same.

'More like who!' Tim said, and I wished the floor would swallow him.

'Interior design,' I said and Jodie laughed. 'You always had an eye for colour.'

'She loved this orange,' Cilla slurred, dropping her hand on to my wrist.

'Furniture,' I said. 'That's what brought me here to Tim.'

'Stinking, mega-rich clients!' Tim smirked. 'I have a bath tub of laundered notes to prove it!'

'I thought they sounded rather sweet,' Josh said, 'your rich clients.'

'Money is a curse!' Cilla declaimed.

'Then Alex is very good at lifting curses,' Steven said.

'Surely to god one can't make a living out of shopping for other people,' Bill said in his dismissive lawyer's voice.

'One can,' I said. 'I do.'

'But you always hated shopping,' Jodie said, wrinkling her lovely eyebrows.

'Only because I was always broke,' I said. 'It's fun with lots of – other people's – money.'

'You should see Jodie's little emporium,' Josh said. 'It's fab. Very ethnic and not a bit hippy, which makes it shine like a beacon in dear old Glastonbury.'

'You have a shop?' I asked her.

'Yes,' she said. 'Third world arty imports, very PC.'

'You'll have to have a look before you go,' Jane said pointedly, 'and you have a lot of catching up to do.'

'Oh, you know each other?' Cilla said, elbows sprawled on the table, chin lolling on her wrists.

'From a long time ago,' I said, and Jodie nodded.

So at least Cilla and Bill didn't know our history.

'Alex knew me when I was married,' Jodie said, 'which was another incarnation.'

'I saw Martin the other week,' Paul said.

'Paul!' Jane said.

'Well, I did,' Paul said.

'Yes, it was Martin, wasn't it,' I said, looking Jodie in the eye.

'It was,' she said.

'Doesn't anyone *stay* married these days?' Cilla brayed, clutching Bill's hand. 'I mean, even when I could *murder* him, I couldn't imagine being without him.'

'I think Jodie tried to stay married,' Tim said, 'didn't you, darling?'

'If anything, for too long,' she said. 'It's very difficult to know when it's over, and mine was definitely over long before I slung him out.'

'God!' Cilla said. 'Slung him out! How dramatic!'

'He had a bit on the side,' Jane said, 'only it wasn't even discreet.'

'She lived over the road,' Jodie said, 'and it was so obvious. I mean, anyone can be unfaithful, but there's a point when it makes you ask what the hell is this about. And it was just a habit, I decided, and not one I wanted to go on with.'

'Usually people have affairs for revenge,' Paul said.

'Paul!' Jane said, flushing.

'Sometimes they fall in love,' Jodie said.

'Oh, love,' Tim said. 'Well, that's an old-fashioned word.'

'It's a beautiful word,' I said.

'Oh, Miss Heartbreak!' he said.

'And are you married? Divorced?' Cilla asked me.

I smiled.

'Alex is a free spirit,' Tim said.

'Recently released,' I said. 'I rather favour forever, but you can't do that all alone.'

'Divorced!' Cilla said. 'I hope you've got a good lawyer.'

'Rather difficult to obtain a divorce when you can't even get married,' I said.

'Darling,' Bill said, 'Alex is *of the other persuasion.*'

'What?' Cilla said, 'Oh god, of course, sorry, how blind of me. You just can't tell these days. Anyway, lesbians are positively chic nowadays!'

'That's the third most popular female fantasy,' Bill said, 'sex with another woman.'

'I can't imagine what they'd do,' Cilla said, predictably.

'Every man here can,' I said, 'if they want to.'

Bill and Paul laughed and Cilla neighed along, and I looked deep into Jodie's eyes. Suddenly it was as if no one else was in the room and a flash of recognition darted between us like the dazzling line drawn by a sparkler on Guy Fawkes night. Recognition? Memory? Or maybe imagination. I tried to think as I lit another cigarette and Tim and Josh cleared plates.

Twenty-four

Some hours later, I was in an apple tree in the orchard at the back of Tim's house, a bottle of champagne wedged in the crook of the branch I was sitting on. I had won my bet about Cilla. After dinner, Tim and Steven had pulled the dressing-up chest into the hall and Tim was demanding charades. Cilla's hot pink and orange jumper was the first to come off, and I nodded to Tim as she revealed a scarlet and black bra and scant wisps of the same colour around her hips. He mouthed 'I-O-U' and stood and watched as Cilla pulled out costume after costume, shrieking and tugging at Bill's shirt.

When I slid out of the room, she was half-way into a lilac crinoline and Bill was cavorting in a Bo Peep frock and bonnet – why do so many straight men seize any opportunity for drag? Jane and Paul seemed to be playing with the Errol Flynn pirate look, and Jodie was holding a Mafioso pinstripe suit against herself. She looked amazing, and I almost joined in, but caught Jane nudging Paul and decided to make my exit.

It was one of those warm, late spring evenings when the stars are so bright and close you feel you could reach out and touch them. I walked away from the laughter and louche jazz until it was only a faint background ripple and leaned against the reassuring firmness of a tree. After a while, the door opened and a bright beam of light splashed out into the cool darkness. I amazed myself by how quickly I climbed that tree and sure enough moments later Steven and Josh were going *woo-hoo!* and *Alex where are yoo hoo* like a pair of demented owls. I stayed perfectly still and after a while they went back in and left me in peace.

When Tim came looking for me, he was more thorough, unlocking the barn for a few minutes. He even stopped right beside my tree, head turning this way and that.

I swigged champagne and lit a cigarette once he had gone. I had some serious thinking to do and, for all my head was fuzzy, the night air was doing a wonderful job of dealing with that. I believe your life flashes in front of your eyes when you are dying: I wanted to re-run the last twenty years slowly and make sense of the feelings surging through me. It felt like the first time I'd met Jodie: then our eyes had searched into each other, as if we had known each other very well a very long time ago. Then, there had been no one else in the room, for all it was a crowded pub. What had we said to each other? How had we wound up holding onto each other in the pub garden, holding on like we were drowning? We hadn't even kissed – then. I remembered that first time of holding her with every cell of my body; god knows how long we stood there. It felt like we were one being, one heartbeat, it felt so right. I can't even say it was sexual. It just was. A moment of feeling so absolutely right. If I had died that moment, I could have told St Peter that my life had been worthwhile.

And then there was light flooding the garden and people everywhere chatting and haw-hawing around the benches and chairs and we weren't holding each other any more, but our eyes kept wandering dizzily towards each other with a thousand questions we couldn't even put into words.

I closed my eyes and could see it so real. She had been wearing a purple T-shirt saying *What About Tibet?* and tie-dye leggings. Her skin felt warm through the cotton and her neck was soft as sun-soaked petals against my cheek.

Voices jerked me into the present; a drunken Steven and Josh *shush shushing* and giggling, hands clasped as they tottered through the grass. They kissed and Josh pushed Steven into the shadows by the barn wall. More kissing and the sound of a zipper as Josh knelt in front of him. Steven spread his arms like Jesus and threw his head back, moaning as Josh's head worked against him. His arms jerked down to grab Josh's hair before he flung him to the ground and tore his jeans away. And now Josh was moaning as his lover ground deep into his ass, one hand on his neck. It was quick and expert, followed by kisses, the combing of hair, and each man checked the other's dress before they strolled back to the party.

I let the velvet darkness settle around me and took my thoughts back to that pub garden all those years ago. I believe everything that happens just keeps on happening in the same place for ever. So Jodie and I would always be holding each other in the darkness, gazing at each other in the unwelcome light. I recalled the moment I realised she was with Martin.

'This is my husband Martin.'

I believe I shook his hand. I am not the hand-shaking kind, but it took me off-guard. After that I felt numb, bereaved; god knows what I said to this unexpected equation of Jodie and Martin. I know I wanted to hit him when he half-slapped her bum, and karate-chop his neck when his mouth kept talking and every word expressed their familiarity and his ownership of her. I remember chatting intently to a rather bemused ex-Forces dyke after that, aware every second of Jodie, hearing her laughter and her words for all we stood at a distance. The Forces dyke told me I looked like I'd had a shock, or else I'd fallen in love and asked me in all seriousness if it had anything to do with her. I remember apologising profusely and then she laughed and tried to guess who it was. Stacey. That was her name. She asked me if I had company for the night and shrugged when I said no and that was the way I wanted it. For all that, she gave me a lift home and we met for drinks a few times. When you're in the heart of the country, dykes and faggots are hard to find, and you never fancy each other, just enjoy the company.

After Jodie, I know I would have gone to bed with Stacey just for the sake of not being alone, but on that evening, when the stars stood still and the moon was gold, and Jodie's whole being filled mine, it would have been sacrilege.

Yes, Stacey took me home and had a coffee, but before we left the pub, I remember saying a warmer goodbye than usual to everyone, and then to Jodie. I turned as I reached the door, and she was looking at me with those wild, green-gold eyes and we just nodded to each other. Like an affirmation.

After that, I knew I belonged to her and she belonged to me. Even if we never saw each other again.

But of course, Glastonbury being such a small series of wheels within wheels, we did.

I drizzled more champagne into my mouth and let it fizz around my tongue while the night played with my memory.

The next time I saw Jodie was in Rico's coffee shop. It was three days after we had held each other so close, and I had been drifting around at some distance from the ground ever since. Everyone in Glastonbury was stoned most of the time, either on hash or whatever energy or synergy was in vogue, so no one noticed. I had been painting some stuff for the festival – what, I can't remember, but it must have been red and yellow and green, because that was the rainbow of colours on my fingers and splattering my baggy overalls. I was sitting at a pavement table drawing when Jodie said hello.

I looked up and felt my heart jerk into a mambo beat.

'Hey', I said, 'hey, hello.'

'Can I join you?' she said, with that voice of hers even more alive than I had been remembering, the sort of voice that holds a bubble of laughter in every syllable. I pushed my clutter onto the pavement and she sat down.

'I've missed you,' she said. 'Do you want a coffee?'

What the hell did I look like? Cheshire Cat grin, eyes like Catherine wheels, hair and clothes streaked with paint, tattered sandals that looped over my big toe, streaks of paint on my ankle. And Jodie? Today her T-shirt said *Boycott China* in gold on scarlet, and a black and scarlet skirt swirled around her to the ankles. I remember diving into her eyes and feeling like that was the only place I wanted to be and I had never belonged anywhere else.

'Gosh, it's good to see you again,' she said.

I had this rush of desire to hold her hand. Just that. And then she clasped mine.

'Weird, isn't it?' she said.

'Yes,' I said, 'weird.'

We just sat there in the sunshine, talking a bit, but mostly just looking into each other's eyes. My whole body was smiling and all I remember of the conversation was that we were going to meet again. Go into the countryside, find a river, find some trees, spend some time. And...

'I don't know what this is about,' she said, 'but I really want to find out.'

'Me too,' I said, and then we had a sort of clumsy daytime friends parting hug. She went one way and I the other, but when I turned to watch her, she had turned as well and we stood for god knows how long. Then nodded.

Yes.

Suddenly the music from the house became louder and light glared into the darkness again. I shifted deeper into the shadows of the tree and blew a little smoke. What fresh hell was this?

A huge raggy shadow blocked the light and lumbered outside. Jesus! Some combination of two people had put on the pantomime horse skin, and the *for god's sake, don't push!* neighing through the night told me that the front end must be Cilla. A bubble of laughter rose in my throat. If she was the head and forelegs then who the hell was the back end? I watched the horse zigzag along the path.

'Bill, stop it!'

'Can't help but appreciate the scenery,' he said, his suave tones a little muffled.

'I can't bloody walk if you've got your hands there!'

'I am a horse's ass,' he said, and I heard the slap of a palm on skin and the horse shrieked with pleasure and reared up.

'You bring out the beast in me,' he said. 'Let's take ourselves for a ride.'

'God, Bill, at least wait until we can get out of this thing!'

'No,' he said, 'this is pure animal lust, my pat-a-cake. Daddy's got a very sweet tooth. Mm-wah! Daddy wants pudding!'

'Daddy can eat as much as he wants,' the front end of the horse said, 'lots and lots of sticky syrup for daddy. And little pudding is all hot and trembly.'

I guessed this was foreplay and just hoped the horse could find it's own field before daddy and little pudding devoured each other.

'Cream and sugar on little pudding? Pleasy please?'

'Oozings and oozums,' the horse's ass promised hoarsely.

They lurched on, polluting the air with saccharine endearments then bumping into my tree. I pinched my cigarette out.

'All syrupy melty now, daddy,' said the horse, now falsetto.

'Daddy's got a big spoon, little puddy.'

The horse collapsed to the ground writhing so that the head was turned 180 degrees and all four legs thrashed.

'Let little syrupy put the big spoon in!'

'Ooh yes, little puddy, right inside the syrup. Yes – ohh, gently little puddy, daddy's going deeper.'

I mean, you read about these things, but even as I doubted what I was seeing and hearing, I thought of the games Fleur and I played. To each their own, I guess. The horse's head bobbed up and down and suddenly the tone changed.

'Daddy's had enough now,' said Bill's voice between gasps and there was an edge of threat in the words.

'Little puddy needs to be gobbled up,' rang out in Cilla's school-mistressy voice, 'Up and up and up, Daddy needs to eat all his pudding up.'

'Bad pat-a-cake,' Bill gasped and I heard his hands start a hard rhythmic slapping while the horse's head jerked backwards and forwards. Suddenly, the whole horse thrashed around and the head lay on the ground while the ass rose into the air.

'Gobble the pudding, daddy, use your big spoon,' Cilla gasped.

And the ass came down very slowly and rose again just as slowly. Over and over again while Cilla whimpered and called Bill *bastard!* All at once, the ass started to jerk harder and faster. A sound like a distant steam train rose into my tree.

'No, no, no.'

'Bad wicked pat-a-cake!'

'No – no – no!'

'Tell Daddy you're sorry!'

'No-no-no, ooooh daddy, I'm sorry, I'm sorry, I'm sorry.'

'Then here's your present, oh darling, oh my god!'

There came a sound like whistling trains colliding in a tunnel and the horse's skin collapsed like a tent. They lay completely still, then started laughing.

'Am I still the best?' Bill said.

'The nonpareil,' Cilla told him. 'Better than anything.'

'Wonder if Tim would lend us this skin,' he said.

'Darling, I'll get one,' she said. 'We'll keep it in the playroom.'

'Love you, oozums,' he said.

'Big daddy,' she said, 'of course you do.'

I watched the horse rearrange itself into its four-legged monstrosity and amble back to the house.

Now, I am not a voyeur by choice. I had actually climbed the tree in Garbo mood. I couldn't imagine Jane and Paul cavorting in the moonlight or – as I suddenly realised I was hoping – Jodie coming to find me.

And something Cilla had just said had hit me like a thousand volts. When Bill had said *Love you, oozums*, she said *of course you do* with the confidence of a benevolent dictator. And – cut out the *oozums* – wasn't that syllable for syllable, tone for tone, exactly what Emilia had said to me when I told her I loved her? Suddenly I saw the entire ghastly pantomime that had been Emilia and me, a grotesque distortion of love playing its cruel and masked charade through days and weeks and months of my life. I had let myself be the Geek in Nightmare Alley, and Emilia was the bottle of rotgut I craved so much I would be a sub-human shit-grovelling sideshow for as long as it took for her to reach my lips.

I knew at that moment that I would rather live in a cave on a trackless mountain than ever see or speak to her again.

Meeting Jodie again had made me remember something as precious and fine as a rainbow. So I stretched and said *hi beautiful, precious girl,* and the words were from her and for her and for me. I could feel moonlight playing a silvery *I love you* all round me. *Dangerous moonlight!* I steadied myself against the fascinating rhythm and took a sip of champagne.

I decided to stay where I was for a while, so that neither Steven nor Josh nor Cilla nor Bill would realise that they had had an audience. And I had only managed to run through the first two times I had seen Jodie. I wanted that past to make sense of the present – god, maybe it would even make sense of the twenty years in between...

Suddenly my cheeks were wet and my tongue found salt water on my lips. And what the hell was that about?

Unbidden, *Visions of Johanna* started to play in my mind.

Memory fast-forwarded to the first time Jodie and I had made love. Not become lovers, because she and I had been lovers from the first time our eyes met and probably many lifetimes before. But the first time our flesh confirmed the love between us, the first time our heartbeats played their own unique symphony, the first

As You Desire Me

time my heart ever beat in time with another, the first time my
whole being was in tune with someone else.

167

Twenty-five

Jodie picked me up the day after Rico's – she had a car and I didn't, something about pollution and anti-technology. I'd had one of those late-night-early-mornings when you find that your wardrobe is a haphazard collection of rags left by some derelict with a sick sense of humour. I'd opted for turquoise satin boots with rainbow laces and deckchair-striped dungarees in blue and white, and some T-shirt with a cute endangered species printed on the front. Hey, the alternative was to look like a flour grader. In those days I hadn't learnt how to dress for the occasion, something about fashion and capitalism.

Jodie was swathed in loose purple and gold, drawstring pants and an embroidered top which clung to her breasts. I watched her hands as she drove – short clean nails, slender fingers, a constellation of freckles on her wrists. A gold band on the third finger of her left hand.

We had been driving for a while before she said, 'Where are we going?'

'I dunno,' I said. 'Um, well, there's a really good wood if we go west a bit.'

'Do you do that?' she said, glancing at me. 'Like directions? I do. It drives Martin mad. I know north, south, east and west. Not road numbers.'

Martin. I swallowed. Told myself this was a friendship and celibacy suited me. A case, at the time, of no choice, or rather, no choice that held any appeal. Stacey had rung me a few times, it's true, probing to find out who my heart belonged to, making it obvious she'd like to come and play, but after the basement years

I'd decided that I was just not that sort of girl. It was easy to hold onto that friendship/celibacy number while we were driving, put the incredible hug, the eye contact, the *knowing* into the realms of fantasy while we sat side by side, although I wanted to grab Jodie's hand so much I had to roll a cigarette instead. In those days I hardly even smoked, just the odd happenstance joint.

She pushed a cassette into the machine – *hope you like it* – and the sound of drums and panpipes filled the car. Pictures of mountain tops and eagles soaring swirled around, and I was in the Andes – Jodie at my side. Just being there and knowing she saw what I saw and felt what I was feeling. No words.

'Like it?' she asked.

'Yeah,' I said, 'lifts you so high.'

We drove on.

'Hey,' I said after a while, 'what about if we do left, left, right?'

She threw her head back and laughed.

'God, Alex,' she said – and I thrilled at her voice pronouncing my name, 'You do that as well? This is weird – incredible.'

She drove fast and just the way it always does, *left, left, right* took us through villages where people are born and never leave, past trees that have seen kingdoms fall, over bridges that have rung to the sound of marching Roman feet.

'And now?' she said. 'Let me decide.'

We were at a crossroads with a grove of silver birch trees to the left, thick Somerset hedgerows to the right, and a signpost to an A road straight ahead. I wanted to go left and sort of held my breath to see where this incredible woman was taking me

Left.

Now she was driving slower and we cruised zigzag bends, undulating gracefully down into a valley and just the way I'd felt it would, the road teamed up with a river and the car came to a halt beside one of those red earth and sand beaches no one ever comes to.

'Yes?' she said, her eyes meeting mine, and I nodded as she turned off the engine.

I wanted so much to hold her, but *Martin* and the gold band on her beautiful finger stopped me.

We walked along the bank, a narrow twisty path, her in front of me, and I was fascinated by the way the purple and gold cotton clung to her shoulders, purple and gold silk shifted as the fabulous curves of her bum moved. The river moved away from the road, and now the ground was dappled shadow, the air smelled green and new as a breeze moved over the corkscrew twists of water.

'Here?' she said, turning to me, and I swear my whole body blushed as she looked at me.

Here was a bank of soft grass woven with ivy and a tree stump and we sat watching the river flow. Suddenly her hand was in mine and then we were in each other's arms and it was just like the pub garden before the lights went on and the human voices woke us from whatever dream we had found.

'It's true, isn't it,' she murmured to me and, whatever she was thinking, I could only say *yes, yes, it's true.*

We looked into each other's eyes again, only this time there was no question, just a sparkle like stars exploding, and our faces came closer and I felt her soft lips questing for mine. My tongue brushed her upper lip and then met the silky warmth of her inner lip and our mouths locked, sucking and caressing the way you would nuzzle the neck of a water bottle after days in a parched desert. My eyes were closed and the heat of her breasts was against mine, one arm round her waist, the other stroking her thigh. And still it was anything but sexual, it was a meeting with the other part of me, as if we'd been parted for an age, exiled from joy for many lifetimes, and suddenly god, or whoever runs the crazy chaos of this universe, had taken pity on the lost and lonely part of me and decided to let me have a taste of heaven.

And I knew without question that she felt the same.

We kissed for a very long time and then she went soft in my arms and drew her head away.

'Jesus,' she said, 'what on earth is this about, Alex? I feel I've known you for a thousand years.'

'I know, ' I said, 'I've been asking myself why and what for and what on earth does it mean ever since – you know – when we held each other.'

'Got any answers?' she said, rubbing her wonderful cheek against mine.

'No,' I said, 'but I've never felt so right.'

'I feel like I've waited for you all of my life,' she said. 'I feel like a string of corny old Motown hits. I don't even know you, but god, Alex, I know you.'

I kissed her brow and her eyelids and plunged my mouth into her neck.

'Darling,' she said, 'darling.'

'Jodie, I love you,' I said. The very words that always led to rejection and ridicule, words I'd sneered at and sworn never to use again. Words that rang sure and true.

'I know you do,' she said, 'and I love you too. God, Alex, I'm in love with you. I haven't been able to think about anything else since I first saw you, you walk the landscape of my dreams. Martin keeps asking me where on earth my head is.'

'Martin,' I said, the first time I'd spoken his name, dread filling me at what the name was to her. 'What about Martin? Jodie, I adore you, I'm just so confused, don't think I'm asking you for answers, but Martin is a reality.'

'I don't know,' she said. 'I love Martin. Just this doesn't seem to have anything to do with Martin. Or with me the way I thought I was. This has never happened to me before, Alex. What about you?'

Twice before this I felt I had been In Love, once with a tutor who played clothes-on games, once with a Ryan O'Neil look-alike who turned out to be gay. With both of those I had the same scenario, hopeless crush and unfulfilled passion, rejection, tears – hence the celibacy. And then there was the crazy basement shit around Zee. But this volcano of every feeling in the world – no.

And this certainty that we were meant for each other and there would be a way – never.

I woke in the chill light just before dawn, my body registering the discomfort of bark against my spine and my hand and wrist stiff around the neck of the half-empty bottle of champagne. I half-slid, half-fell to the ground, and rubbed my hand in the wet grass, pushed my palms against my face and let the cold dew wake me.

The house was silent, the hall empty, the debris of the night before predictable – candle stumps, empty glasses, piles of clothes dumped here and there.

Everyone had gone or gone to bed, and I made coffee and took it back outside.

It amazed me how high I had climbed the night before – I guess alcohol and the need to be alone had fuelled my muscles beyond their usual capacity. I strolled through the orchard and leaned on the fence, watching three horses canter through the low strands of mist, their hooves spraying up rainbows.

I'd been horse-riding with Jodie as well.

She was a big woman, comfortable with her body. I was more than comfortable with her body. A lot of big people always seem to be pulling bits in, or wearing monotonous black. But Jodie lived in the warm curves of her skin, and her whole body shivered with delight when I stroked her, fascinated by every pore. When we lay together her arm was heavy across my breasts, and when she held me, I felt tiny and so cherished.

My am self started jeering at these tender memories. As in *bitch, it's been twenty years, who says you've even crossed her mind?* I don't like my am self, excellent though she is at pouring cold water from a great height onto my dreams. But without her sarcasm there would have been many days when I wouldn't even have got out of bed through the psychodrama that was Emilia, and it was her cattle-prod subtlety that had lashed me to get up, get fine, get funky and get out to Chris, to Miss X, to the night-club where the gold-streaked blonde had danced with me and had my clit stiffen and swell like a gypsy's clothes peg.

I sipped coffee and lit a cigarette, coughing as the horses blew noisy breaths that sounded like laughter. I got some apples from the house and the horses came over to me and nuzzled from my palm. I knew I would end up living in the country some day and it was moments like this that confirmed it: stillness and an air of something wonderful about to happen – like the sudden sunrise that swept rich pink through the mist and simply took my breath away. I sat on the fence and stretched in the first rays of warmth.

Maybe I would hit the road today, I thought. After all, my business was more than satisfactorily done.

Is it?

Christ! The am *gauleiter* sounded very insistent. I listened, but no more came, just a picture of Jodie in last night's candlelight and her eyes mesmerising me.

The grey horse nudged my knee and I rubbed his ears and waxy mane. Then I smiled and slung one leg over his back and urged him forward with my knees. Away we went, at a canter first, then as we topped the first ridge of the field, I felt his strong sides pulse against my thighs, eager for more, and so we galloped swerving at the hedge and back up the hill again. The other horses joined us and the air stung my face and blew away all last night's cobwebs and stiffness.

No, I wouldn't leave today.

There was unfinished business with Jodie and I didn't have a clue what it was, but all of me knew that we had been together in too many beautiful yesterdays to walk away again without something – whatever – being spoken and acknowledged.

Might just be a service of remembrance…

So be it.

…or a sentimental journey.

My horse slowed at the top fence and I jumped to the ground and scraped the heel of my hand along his neck.

'You want a date tomorrow?' I said.

Talking to yourself, Alex?

Someone's got to do it.

Tim was unlikely to emerge before mid-afternoon, so I showered and changed. – suddenly looking at my unruffled bed and the card on the pillow.

> *Beulah's Caprice*
> *Unique Arts and Crafts*
> *Jodie D'Acosta*

And a Glastonbury phone number.

So Jodie had gone back to her first surname. I sat on the bed and looked at the golden square of card. And Jodie – the name she said she'd always wanted; it felt much more her than Joanna, which she thought was rather school prefect.

'When I've got the nerve to be me, I'll only answer to Jodie.'

We'd been lying in bed together when she said that; I was resting on the glorious solid warmth of her body and I called her Jodie from then on, whenever we were alone.

And Beulah!

We'd done the camp Mae West number on that one, peeling grapes and feeding each other the sweet, wet flesh. One time, I made a path of peeled grapes from her breast to her navel and down to the luxuriant red-gold jungle of her hair and I traced along the sweetness with my tongue and lips, and her skin was sweeter than wine. Beulah is a name for the promised land and as I read her business card, my heart raced, pumping a thousand hopes and questions with every beat.

Coffee.

Back in the dazzling day, I switched my phone on and punched her number. Before I could ring, messages flashed on the screen. Fleur – hoping my trip was fab, and expressing a wish to suck me till I screamed. Chris – wondering where I was, and was I aware that I might have competition? Fleur – wanting to talk, things happening with Chris. And Nell – Nell? – saying here was her number again, in case I'd lost it. Nell – the nightclub blonde.

And Emilia, saying she would always hold me dear and we had something so special.

I pressed *Delete*.

It all seemed like a world away.

I rang Jodie and drew on my cigarette like it was oxygen.

Twenty-six

'Alex,' she said and sounded pleased.

'Yeah,' I said, 'sorry I didn't say goodnight. I went to sleep in a tree.'

She laughed.

'I just thought,' I said, 'I mean, you can't really talk at one of Tim's dinner parties.'

'You want to talk to me?' she said.

'Yes,' I said, 'I do – do you?'

'That's why I left my card,' she said. 'I'm not very convinced about Tim's ability to pass on messages.'

'Right,' I said, and another text message bleeped on the screen. I ignored it.

'What are you doing for breakfast?' she said.

'You tell me,' I said.

Moments later, I was driving the high-banked lanes towards Glastonbury. I read the text that had come through while Joanna – Jodie – talked to me.

Chris again: *Ring me or forget it.*

Well, hush mah mouf – whether it was a hangover talking, the am *gauleiter* or the real me – I just couldn't give a shit.

I pushed a Mozart tape into the machine.

Chris who?

Jodie's house was on the outskirts of Glastonbury and, to reach the front door, you climbed a curve of mossy steps with the scent of lavender dripping through the air. It had the look of a building slipping into the earth, with golden flowers cascading round the trellised porch.

Number Seven.

'I'm here,' she said, as I reached the door, and I turned to the familiar sound of her voice.

She was sitting at a wooden table on the grass by the side of the house, her feet up on the bench. I walked over and sat opposite her. The morning sun made a halo through her hair and our eyes met briefly, curious, then guarded.

'You drinking coffee these days?' she asked.

'By the bucket,' I said.

'Remarkable,' she said. 'You were so purist when I knew you before. And you're driving! Alex meets the twenty-first century!'

I laughed and watched her easy walk across the lush grass. The peace in her garden wrapped around me like coming home. A dragonfly looped the loop in magnificent stripes of chocolate and gold, its clear wings with their stained glass veins sparkling as it circled the sacred space. Lavender, hollyhocks, marigolds, sweet william – all the flowers of a cottage garden jigsaw from childhood. Only there was no little old, long-skirted granny at the door, just Jodie in a flowing kaftan of russet and lilac putting a dark cafetière on the table beside me. I felt the heat of her body as she moved behind me and it made me dizzy.

'What have you been up to?' she said, sitting opposite me again.

Twenty crazy years helter-skeltered through my mind. Oh shit!

'Stupid question,' she said, 'and none of my business. Talk to me Alex, you said you wanted to talk.'

'I do,' I said, 'only now – you know how now just seems like, well hey, this is lovely and god, there's a lot to say, but I can't think of a thing.'

She tossed back her thick hair and smiled.

'This *is* a moment,' she said, 'I know.'

Did she? Did she know that I never thought this moment would come?

'Never thought we'd see each other again' she said. 'It was weird when you left. Do you want to talk about that?'

'Do you?' I said, just wanting to hold her and make all the crazy times simply vanish.

'Alex, Alex,' she said, 'you still do that. Not fair. Question for a question? Answer mine first.'

'Yes, I do,' I said, 'very much. Never talked to anyone about that day I went. Well, small talk to Smallboy – you know.'

'Me neither,' she said. 'Well, a little bit. To Jane. She wanted to hit you. That's why I came last night.'

'You knew I'd be there?'

'Yes. I work a bit with Tim, and Jane and he are forever going to auctions.'

'Why did you come?'

'To stop Jane hitting you, Alex,' she said seriously, 'and to see you again. I thought if I don't then I'll never see you again, and maybe it's time. Don't look so scared, Beulah, it doesn't suit the rather urbane self you seem to be these days.'

'OK, Beulah,' I said, 'and I'm not scared. Just Tim didn't tell me you'd be there and I didn't know what to say. Or do.'

'You did fine,' she said, 'especially with Cilla. She thinks you're a darling. She was braying at Bill to have you come and do their mansion when they finally left.'

'What time was that?'

'Four?' she said. 'After that, I gave up on you coming back and just checked you hadn't gone to bed – that's when I left my card. Thank you for ringing.'

'And you for leaving your card,' I said. There was an edge of formality between us but it felt like that was OK, as if somehow we had been given this open-ended time and what we did with it was completely up to us.

I drank coffee and it tasted good.

'So tell me what happened twenty years ago,' she said, 'if you can remember.'

'Miaow,' I said, 'fair enough, Jodie. OK. Well, it was a Wednesday.'

'It was,' she said.

'You'd been weird,' I said. 'Well, maybe you weren't, but I thought you were. Sort of rushing off early, and going places without me. And without Martin. I felt – feared – you'd gone off me. Tim might be a lousy agony aunt, but he was there and he'd been there when you weren't. I was just – well, a mess.'

'You?' she said, 'A mess? You were always so lovely to me.'

'I was crying all the time you weren't there,' I said, forcing a laugh. 'Tim decided I should go away and start living. He said you'd never leave Martin and I said you would, and he got very fierce and protective. So he booked me a flight for that Wednesday and sent me off to San Francisco. He said he'd tell you I had to go and, if anything looked hopeful, he'd call me. Only when he called me, he said it really was no go and he kept finding bits of courier stuff for me all over. I hardly saw England for years.'

'Oh,' she said, 'I see.'

A muscle played in her cheek as if she was holding in words that were longing to spill out towards me.

'So that was my Wednesday,' I said. 'Blind with tears and gin all the way across the Atlantic. Weepy Wednesday, the worst one of my life.'

She reached over and took my hand and I could see tears in her eyes.

'Alex, Alex,' she said, 'I'm so sorry.'

'You're sorry?' I said. 'I was the one who left. Jodie – what are you sorry for?'

'That Wednesday, I went to our place,' she said, 'you know – that tree where I always picked you up and you weren't there and you didn't come. And I drove all over, even out to Tim's, and no one was there. I was frantic. I had something really important to tell you, you see. When I did get hold of Tim the next day, he said you'd gone, and I can't even remember what I said.'

'He said you'd said that perhaps it was as well,' I said.

'I probably did. You see, why I'd gone off on my own – well, Alex, we were having a baby.'

'Martin always wanted to be a father,' I said, shaking.

'Oh, listen to me, Alex,' she said, '*we* wasn't me and Martin. You were my lover then and for me that was forever.'

'Jodie,' I said, 'don't tell me parthenogenesis. We? How?'

'I slept with Martin,' she said. 'I had to. He was getting very suspicious, thought I had a man somewhere. And I loved him and he was acting so hurt. I couldn't tell you we slept together because – well, I couldn't. It felt like being unfaithful to you, to me, to us. That bloody Wednesday I was going to tell you about the baby and I thought you'd go mad – I didn't know what you'd do.'

'A baby?' I said, stunned, 'What happened?'

'She's nineteen now. She's at dancing school,' Jodie said. 'I called her Alice. You'd like her.'

'Of course I'd like her,' I said.

'And she's got your eyes,' Jodie said. 'Martin thinks they're from his side, his blue-eyed mother, but they're not. They're yours. Every time I looked at her I saw you. Silly, I suppose. To hell with silly, I knew it was true.'

'Show me a picture,' I said, feeling a melting through me like an ice-cap slipping into warm waves, drinking in the beauty of Jodie and then, in a breathtaking rush, I was weeping in her glorious, strong arms.

Twenty-seven

I held her and she held me, with one hand on the back of my head the way you carry a baby. My face was crushed against the cotton of her blouse and, god, she smelled like spring meadows in sunshine. I felt her heart thud against my cheek, and I struggled to stand, needing to hold all of her next to me. The pulse in the soft skin of her neck beat against my brow like a butterfly. Her breath caressed my ear and we were both shaking.

'Let's both sit,' she said and the words shivered through her shoulders and mine as we stumbled to the bench.

I knew that – for me – nothing had changed for all the time we'd been apart, and my head fought this sudden unexpected truth. It was like a dream, this wonderful closeness. A wave of sheer love swept through me and swept me off my feet the moment we held each other. And it was nothing to do with sex – the focus was complete fulfilment.

Jodie believed she'd been my mother in a past life, although we'd both laughed at the feeling between us in this one – anything but maternal or daughterly. But sometimes when she held me, when I nuzzled her breasts, I felt so small and secure I knew she was right. Then, there was the life when we'd been husband and wife although we could never work out who had been what.

But this was this life and what we did with it was up to both of us.

We'd often talked about it, Jodie with her fears, me with mine, talked about it to an edge where we almost flew into our dreams.

And in this peaceful garden, as never before between us, the moment was now.

I could have drawn away and made some flip comment about still being a little bit drunk; I could have lit a cigarette and turned it round to polite chit-chat; I could have wept, laughed, run away down the path and into my car and back to all the things my life had become since I last held Jodie. But all I wanted to do was stay in her arms, with none of the years that had passed without her having happened, and not another second of my life without her being a remote possibility.

Then, as our bodies shifted ever so slightly, and the heat of her skin kissed mine through the illusion that was our clothes, I wondered what she was feeling, and if she was wondering the same. I breathed in her skin and she shuddered in my arms.

It was the hardest thing I'd ever done when I drew my face away from her neck to look into her eyes and, god, she was crying and so was I as my lips brushed the tears from her cheek, and her soft mouth smooched my eyelids.

'You wanted to see a photo,' she said, and I kissed her parted lips, drawing the soft wetness of her mouth against my tongue.

'I do,' I said, 'but not now – only want to see you, Jodie.'

'It's weird,' she said. 'It's like you've never been away.'

'Maybe I haven't,' I said. 'Feels like that to me too.'

She drew her head back slightly and her eyes were laughing.

'But you have been away,' she said. 'All over the planet and very successful too. This feels beautiful, but Alex, what's happening in your life?'

'You,' I said and I meant it with all my heart.

'God,' she said, 'you do the worst lines and I love it. No, Alex, tell me. Tim gave the impression of your busy, busy life, and you were talking in smart riddles last night. I kept looking at you and seeing you how you were, and you sounded so blasé I wondered if you were still you. And you are you, only with everything life's been doing to you since we were last together.'

I didn't want to tell her anything at all – not Fleur, not Chris,

not Nell, none of the flings and one-night stands and affairs and
flying fucks that had filled the thousands of days we'd been apart.
And what else had I been doing? Shopping for the rich and bored.
I looked away from her slightly.

'OK,' she said, 'I guess that says it's none of my business. And
if it isn't, then maybe I'm none of yours. Alex, I'm not exactly
naive. You must be involved, I can't see you being on your own.'

'It's not that,' I said, looking deep into her eyes.

*It's just that everything I've been so busy with seems so tawdry and
I feel so goddamned ashamed and if you knew what my life was like
would you be holding me so close, my darling, my angel.*

'Tell me what those eyes are saying,' she said, stroking my hair.

'Don't know how to start,' I said.

'Just talk,' she said.

Well, I just didn't want to. What the hell had any of that time
without her to do with now? The only talking I wanted was about
now – and that seemed so scary, so fragile, precious and magical,
like a soap bubble blown into the air by a child. It felt like any
words could break its rainbowed surface and I couldn't bear to
think about that.

'Jodie, darling,' I said, 'I really don't want to talk about the
past.'

Her eyes held me. 'I don't want you to either,' she said. 'I don't
want there to be a past to talk about, because then we'd have to
talk about now – you know? Not just be.'

'Don't you want to talk about now?'

'No,' she said, 'because now is you and your flash car, which
means you'll be driving away to your life and that's miles away
and I don't even want to think about that.'

'That's not the now I want to talk about,' I said, holding her
strong hand in mine, 'I don't know what this is about but, god,
woman, I never did. I just know that I'm the fool who left you
years ago and I wish I never had and there's not a damn thing in

my life that means enough to go back to.'

'God,' she said, 'can I believe that?'

I kissed her.

'Yes,' I said, 'if that's what you want.'

'Is it what you want, Alex?' she said.

'Yes,' I said, 'that's what I want whether you want it or not and I hope you do.'

She wrapped her arms around me again and sighed like a contented puppy who's found the warmest and softest rug in the world.

'What do you want right now?' she said.

'I want to be somewhere with you alone,' I said, 'I want to love you forever. And you?'

'Yes,' she said, 'let's find somewhere.'

Jodie's bed was wide, with white sheets and a cover stroked with clear lilac. Her windows were wide open and a breeze shifted snowy veils of cotton studded with purple and lilac flowers. Her bed was golden wood and we stood together for a moment, our hands clasped. Without a word, we shed clothes and she lay down and drew me in beside her, tucking the cover round my shoulders. I closed my eyes and let the wonderful sensation of her naked body fill and thrill me.

Twenty-eight

We lay there silent for a long time. I became aware of a web of tension that had lived so long under my skin that it had become part of me – and here, in Jodie's bed, every taut thread of it started to relax. First across my shoulders where the silk of her inner arm was so warm, so close that it was as if we had melted into each other. Her hand stroked my shoulder and every cell crackled to life and heat under her fingertips. My arm was around her ribs and I held onto her like I was drowning. Gradually, my spine pulsed to a sweet and gentle contentment and an elastic freedom stretched right to my toes. My arm relaxed and I let my hand hover just above her skin and she drew me even closer. It felt like heaven.

I pushed her thighs apart and climbed to rest there, with my head on her breasts, looking up at her wonderful face, every love song the world has ever written playing through my head. Kissed her chin, kissed her cheek, my lips becoming one with her neck.

I loved Jodie's neck; she joked that I must have been a vampire. God! How I'd longed to bruise her neck with my teeth and how careful we'd been because of Martin. And now there was no Martin to walk on eggshells around, I didn't want to bruise her, just cup her face in my hands and be inside her glorious eyes.

'Darling,' she said, 'darling.'

Our lips fluttered over each other's radiant faces before we snuggled – oh god, how? – even closer.

'I am you,' I said.

'I am you,' she said. 'I'm yours, Alex, always have been.'

'I'm yours,' I said. 'That's forever.'

Her lips pressed onto my brow, not a kiss, just so close, so tender.

'I feel like saying *where were we?*' she said. 'This is so now, Alex, and I've dreamed of you so many times. Always wanting you close, so close to me.'

'You still do it,' I said, 'say what I'm thinking.'

I cupped my hand round her breast and nuzzled her soft nipple.

'You always do what I'm wanting you to do,' she said, sighing and stroking my shoulders.

'Like nothing has changed,' I said. 'Your fingers on my shoulder. God, woman, I've missed you.'

'Every day?' she said mocking me gently.

'Yes,' I said, 'even days when you didn't cross my head, now I know it was you that was missing.'

She pulled away from me slightly and tipped my chin, looking me in the eyes.

'I like that,' she said, smiling, 'but I hope I didn't, oh, you know, stop you from living, Alex.'

'I've been living,' I said, 'the fast lane, my angel, very exciting. Been doing what I would have envied in someone else. Just all seems like a rather silly play now I'm here where I've wanted to be all the time.'

I stroked her midriff and ruffled my thumb in her warm springy hair.

'Knockin' on heaven's door,' I said.

'God,' she said, 'I couldn't play Bob Dylan after you.'

'Me neither,' I said. 'Well, let's be honest – too much brandy and I could play nothing else.'

'Always be honest with me, Alex,' she said. 'It's what we always had and, even if you think I won't like it, always tell me the truth. I can deal with it, darling. I'm a big girl now.'

'You're my girl,' I said.

'My baby girl,' she said, kissing me, her tongue exploring my lips as her eyes travelled into mine and my heart lurched.

'My crazy woman,' she said.

'You're my everything,' I said, and I knew it was true.

'So what do we now?' she said, holding my face in her strong hands. 'Apart from make love? I so want to make love with you but I don't want you to go away ever again either.'

'You know what you used to say to me?' I said. 'I may get some of the words wrong, but you said if only you'd met me when what you did only affected you and there were no responsibilities and commitments and so there was no hurt? And you meant Martin. And now there isn't Martin, Jodie, so what was your *if only*? I was always too scared to ask.'

'That if only none of the rest of my life was happening then we'd be together forever, Alex,' she said. 'That was my *if only* and you know it. And now there's no *if only* – for me, anyway. But what about you? Is there an *if only*?'

I tucked my head into her shoulder and closed my eyes.

'My *if only* is if only I'd hung around here and not just pissed off,' I said. 'If only I'd had the nerve to tell you what I wanted and ask if you wanted it, too! I don't have an *if only* now. I have business to finish – the Turners' mansion. I have a flat to do something with. A few people to say goodbye to. And some *au revoirs*. Can do most of that by phone.'

'And then what?' she asked, kissing my eyelids and cheeks urgently. 'What do you want then, Alex?'

'And then Norway,' I said, 'or here. Or anywhere so long as you're there. And forever. I can't be without you any more, Jodie, I really don't think I could stand it. I don't want to. Jesus, it's so hard to say what I want.'

'Is that in case you think I don't want it as well?' she asked me and her eyes shone with tears.

We kissed and it was oxygen.

'Alex, you bloody fool,' she said, 'it's all I ever wanted. If you'd put your foot down years ago Martin would have been history and we would have had our history already. And more to come.'

'I couldn't,' I said. 'You remember when I tried to? And you got all frantic and said was I trying to make you choose, because you just couldn't?'

'Jesus,' she said, 'I did, didn't I? And then Martin got all heavy, after you'd gone, and said I had to choose – was I his wife, or did I want to do my own thing? There was a lot of pressure because I was pregnant and he went all macho and great provider and taking the piss out of me wanting to do my own thing, the business and that. And he was a good guy, Alex, he really was. It would have been so simple if he'd been a bastard.'

'So what did you do?' I said.

'I slung him out,' she said. 'So I was all the bastards and bitches, not him. I still had this absurd idea that you'd be back, darling. And he got really vile and questioned if he was Alice's father. Alex, you have no idea. He couldn't seem to accept that I just didn't want him any more and there wasn't another man. Then he would be lovely to me sometimes and that made it worse. I just wanted you and I couldn't find you. I felt like a wolf howling at the moon.'

'That eclipse,' she said, 'the year that you left – you remember? I walked to the Tor and sat all night begging the stars, or god, or anything that was listening, to bring you home to me.'

'I was on a ferry,' I said, 'going to Capri for some dodgy diamond and lapis heirlooms for Tim. I stayed on deck all night and watched the full moon and then those moments of total darkness during the eclipse. A ring of silver fire, Jodie. Like a fairground hoop that almost settles on the prize, only when it stops spinning, it hasn't? And I was drinking Strega out of the bottle and wanting to feel so drunk I stopped missing you, only it wouldn't hit the spot. I wanted to ring you, only by the time there was a phone it was bright Mediterranean daylight and I jeered myself out of it.'

'I drank a bottle of sweet martini at the Tor that night,' she said, 'and I was sober as a judge. So we were both drinking sickly sweetness at the same time.'

I knew if we checked dates that all the nights I'd shot out of sleep, or walked some foreign shore while the moon rose and set, or found myself awake and weeping – all these would be the times she had been calling out for me – and the times my soul had been raging at the universe for the lack of her.

'I kept a diary that year,' I told her. 'Never done it before or since, but it seemed the only route to sanity without you.'

'I want to read it,' she said. 'I kept a bloody diary too.'

'I'll find it when I pack up my flat,' I said.

'Let's read both of them.' she said, 'and then burn them.'

'Right,' I said.

We moved a little so that our skin registered the sheer bliss of each other, where we had been melting into one. It was vital to feel our separateness, and life itself to become one.

Jodie's skin became satin on her belly, her thighs were silk, her neck was swansdown, her damask breasts rippled into nipples of crêpe de chine. My fingertips drew the finest stitchwork of sheer adoration all over her. She sighed like a gentle breeze ruffling fine fabric at an open window in a summer dawn.

'I have to ask you,' she said, 'because I feel I have to. Is there anyone around you these days, Alex, like – um – in terms of love?'

Fleur? Emilia? Chris? Nell? The names curled up and dropped like the petals when it's time to bin a bouquet that's been kept too long, and the stems have started to make slime of the water.

'No,' I said, 'but do I have to ask you that too?'

'Thank god, no,' she said. 'I just couldn't bear for there to be any hurt caused because of us. And that's what screwed it up last time. I just wondered when you said there were goodbyes and *au revoirs*. And, oh Christ, Alex, what Tim said, well, implied.'

'Which was?' I said, caressing her navel with my tongue.

'That you were this rampant, libidinous new woman, very Y2K, knocking the Bridget Jones type into a cocked hat.'

Her voice was suddenly distant and hard and for all the words were light and clever, I could feel her heart thundering and her fingers gripped my shoulders.

'I've had my moments,' I said. 'I can't lie to you, Jodie. You want a blow-by-blow account? If you do, you can have it. But all I want to say, darling, is that I've had my moments. But this moment is ours and this moment is now.'

'Because you'd better be sure,' she said and each word came out strong. 'You'd better be so sure, Alex, and if you have any doubt at all, then you'd better look at it. My whole life has waited for you and then I've waited for this moment. And I'm sure.'

'And I'm sure,' I said.

'Well, that's all right then,' she said, and her voice was shaking.

Our lips met, and our bodies fused together and, for the first time in twenty years, I was making love with Jodie.

No – I was with Jodie, in *Love*, and we were making *Love*.

Twenty-nine

When the evening came, we talked about eating, but neither of us wanted to get out of bed. We talked about drinking, and ditto. It was impossible not to be touching her, unthinkable to let her out of my sight. Finally, almost hysterical with hunger and the mad scientist rumblings our stomachs were making, which we both disowned, and laughing as we pressed an ear to each other's belly, we decided to go to the kitchen together and bring whatever we could find back upstairs.

It was lovely to walk downstairs naked, holding Jodie's hand, kissing her shoulder at the turn of the stairs.

'And you'd better ring Tim,' she said. 'I don't want him ringing us.'

She'd ignored the phone all day and, while she opened cupboards and giggled, I made the call. Just told Tim he'd see me when he saw me, and he asked was it Jodie and I told him to piss off and be psychic elsewhere.

Back in bed, Jodie spread a white silk shawl on the duvet by way of a tablecloth.

'Thai bites,' she said, 'rice crackers, strawberries, houmous, sesame bread sticks, raspberries, olives, baby figs – god, Alex, this is all a bit healthy.'

'Grapes?' I asked her and she kissed me gently on the mouth, then hard as if she was starving, gripping my face in her lovely hands.

'And New Zealand fizz,' she said. 'It's all I ever drink.'

'It's all we ever drank,' I said. 'Do you know how wonderful you are?'

Her eyes widened and sparkled the way they did when she was near to ecstasy. Like galaxies explode – stars are born in the deep space of swirling desire. Jodie's eyes took me floating in a miasma of colours so vivid, so delicate that I was aware of every cell of both our bodies, as if I were a macrocosm, a dazzling flurry of lights in an infinite chain of life surging through us.

Electric – a lightning storm over an ocean played slow.

'Our glasses,' she said. 'Do something with that bottle.'

I traced the clear stem as she reached towards me.

'The same glasses?' I said, my fingertips thrilling as the crystal rang.

'Yes,' she said. 'I stashed them to stop myself throwing them up the wall when it got too bad. I never thought we'd be using them again, and I could never have used them with anyone else.'

The cork edged out the bottle then flew with a bang. I filled both glasses, and the bubbles sparkled like her smile.

'To us,' I said, and the crystal rang clear as a windchime as we toasted here and now and what we both were dreaming.

'Forever,' she said, and my heart lurched with certainty.

'Always,' I said and we drank, gazing at each other, unblinking.

We ate, throwing strawberry leaves on the floor, spitting olive pits over the end of the bed, sesame seeds scattered in the sheets.

'I love making a mess with you,' she said.

'Your car was a tip when we'd made love,' I said.

'The man at the car valet place made a bloody fortune out of me,' she said.

I sucked her strawberry-stained fingertips and stretched out as she cleared the debris of our picnic to the floor. I cupped her heel in my hand and smooched her toes, sucking each one and watching her lovely body arch with pleasure. Her hair felt warm and glorious as she bent her head to my foot and the heat and wetness of her tongue worked on my instep, she licked my foot from ankle to toe and grazed her teeth against my skin.

'Jodie, I love you,' I said, clasping her calf to my breasts.

'I love you, Alex,' she said.

Maybe it was morning, I don't know, but I found myself waking up beside her beautiful, gentle softness, with the strength of her arms around me. Her hand was on my head and I snuggled closer.

'Baby, you've been sleeping,' she said.

'And I didn't want to miss a moment,' I said, kissing her. 'Darling, did you sleep?'

'Dozed,' she said, 'but I love to watch you sleeping. It makes me feel so protective, so trusted.'

I dipped my mouth to her breast and her nipple filled my mouth as I sucked.

'Gorgeous,' she said, 'just perfect. Hey, darling, do you want breakfast?'

'I want you,' I said.

'Good,' she said, 'because I want you too.'

'Is there a but there?' I said, wrapping her close into me.

'Only it's the day after tomorrow,' she said. 'I have a shop somewhere and you have pianos and sculptures and we're going to have to deal with them sometime. Alex…'

'What?' I said, for a grey shadow crossed her eyes as she looked away from me.

'If it's just now, it's OK,' she said. 'I mean, if this was just a moment – while you were sleeping, oh god, I just thought, well, I'm happy now. And happy for as long as you can be here with me. I watched the sun rise while you were sleeping and every second is so precious and beautiful, but god, Alex…'

I turned her face to look at me.

'You should have woken me for the sunrise,' I said, 'but we can see tomorrow's, and watch the sunset – together.'

But there was a tension in her, a watchfulness in her eyes.

'Tell me,' I said.

'It's OK if you want to go,' she said.

'It's not OK for your tears,' I said. 'Crazy woman, I don't want to go anywhere. I told you, I have to tidy things up and then – hey – you do want to be with me, don't you? I guess I should say it's OK if you don't. But it isn't. Unless you do?'

'I just don't want to be too hopeful,' she said. 'Defences, I guess. What if you go home to tidy things up and then something happens and you don't come back?'

'Well, come with me,' I said, 'and then we can run away together.'

She relaxed and sighed as we kissed.

'I'll make coffee,' she said. 'Let's have coffee in the garden.'

She threw a silk dressing gown at me and slid into a kaftan and this time we went downstairs side by side, arms round each other.

I switched my phone on outside. Tim. Mrs Turner. The estate agent. They might as well have been on another planet.

Jodie came towards me, and my heart lurched – it was as strong as the first time we had seen each other. No, stronger. And every second, as I watched the curve of her fingers on the handle of the cup, the light flicker of muscle in her forearm, her strong brown wrists – every second I was hers, more and more. Looking into her eyes, I felt everything change a gear, like a space ship breaking through gravity, roaring into eternity.

'Let's plan,' I said to her.

'Yes,' she said. 'We never could do that before, could we?'

'Only dream,' I said, lighting a cigarette.

'You haven't smoked in forty-eight hours,' she said.

'Better things to do with my mouth,' I said. 'Let's plan, Jodie, I want to do this.'

'The efficient Alex Scott,' she said. 'So what have you planned? Who were the calls for?'

I told her and she smiled.

'You do mean it, don't you?' she said, nodding.

'Jodie – I have a superstition – the one place I would never go to was Norway because that's ours,' I said. 'Shall we go to Norway?'

'Jesus,' she said, 'you remember everything, don't you?'

'There are ferries from North Shields,' I said. 'I used to go and watch them when I was near there. Have a good cry. I want to be walking onto a ferry with you, holding your hand and going to Norway.'

'Let's do it then,' she said. 'I'll get the shop covered – how long for?'

'Dunno,' I said. ''Till we've spent all the Turner money?'

'OK,' she said.

'When do we go?' that we said together.

And decided it would have to be a Wednesday. Tomorrow was Wednesday.

'A week tomorrow?' I said.

'That's eight sleeps,' she said. 'I used to say that to Alice when she was little. She was so impatient, like you. And now I feel like I'm the impatient one.'

'Me too,' I said.

It was the hardest thing in the world to drive away, and eight sleeps felt like forever. But as Jodie said, tomorrow was seven sleeps and then it was six, and so soon after that no sleeps at all, it would be sunrise on the day we would meet at the ferry and run away just like we'd always planned.

And never say goodbye to each other again.

Thirty

I rang Jodie as I hit the motorway. It seemed like an age since I'd seen her and touched her, and heard her wonderful voice.

'My hands smell of you,' she said. 'I miss you like crazy. I'm in the shop and I just can't focus, and darling, there you are, driving.'

'Something's driving for me,' I said. 'I don't have any bones. Jodie, I'm in love with you, I find I'm doing ninety, then I'm doing fifty. Jodie, you blow every fuse I've ever had.'

'Good,' she said. 'It feels like I'm walking on a rainbow, and god, Alex, it's so real. I feel so alive.'

'Ditto,' I said.

We talked for the next hundred miles, punctuated by her customers and the odd patrol car in my rear mirror. Then we decided to take a break so I could burn the road, get back and get everything cleared and sorted. The traffic was building up and moments later there was a cloudburst and everything slowed as the sodden air crackled with danger. Lorries backwashed my vision and all I wanted to do was turn back and just let everything sort itself. Can't do that. The next week might be the longest of my life, but it was where my life began.

I stopped for coffee after a while to let the sky clear a little.

Messages flashed on my phone.

Just let me know you're OK.

Fleur.

I need to know you're OK. Know my decision was right but I need to have you in my life.

Emilia.

I knew I would ring Fleur. She had always been a lady and

199

always treated me with impeccable courtesy. I owed it to her to tell her why I was simply going to vanish. And Emilia could simply go to the twisted circle of hell where games players scheme and destroy, and teach them a few new tricks. God help Marcie, still strung up and helpless, and god help the next fool who fell under her spell.

Thinking about it, Fleur would be the first person I had ever given any kind of explanation to in all the times I had got up and gone. I wondered how she would take it, whether our vow to avoid Love was true. Whether she would give me hell, and maybe that was why I'd never done any explaining to anyone before. Cowardice and an aversion to scenes? Who cared? For the first time in as long as I could remember I knew what I wanted, absolutely.

I punched Fleur's number.

'Alex,' she said, sounding genuinely pleased, 'I thought you must be all right, since you didn't feature in the Sunday scandal sheets. Where are you?'

'On the way back,' I said. 'Are you free this week?'

'I can always find a window for you, dear heart,' she said, 'but you sound rather serious and preoccupied. Is everything OK?'

'Very,' I said, 'just been driving through shitty bloody weather.'

'Well, take care,' she said. 'I was wanting to talk to you, anyway – developments, you know.'

'Chris?' I said, suddenly hoping that particular liaison had taken off to divert her.

'Oh god,' she said, 'dear Chris. No, my sweet. Nothing like Chris. But definitely something I wanted to say face to face.'

She wouldn't say more and we arranged dinner for the next night. And after that dinner, it would be five sleeps.

And when I rang Jodie it had stopped raining and she was still in love with me and I drove along under a triple rainbow.

Thirty-one

The estate agent met me at my flat, and while she whisked around making notes, I called Marjorie Turner.

'I've been frantic,' she said. 'George has a lot of important people coming at the weekend – the weekend, Alex. I don't know what to do. I love everything we've planned, but there's no time.'

'That's fine,' I said – nothing could faze me now I was with Jodie. 'I like a challenge. Your piano and the statues arrive tomorrow morning, the furniture arrives Thursday afternoon, there isn't a problem. We can work round the clock.'

'But there's so much more,' she said. 'I can't see how it'll happen, but you seem so confident.'

'There's nothing that can't be done,' I said, my mind switching into overdrive, 'But you'll have to let me just do it, Marjorie. Plants and things. We've talked, but you'll just have to trust me with such short notice. Now – have you got your needlepoint in frames? Have you got your catering sorted out?'

'Oh yes,' she said. 'Yew frames, just like you said – that I can do and the man was very complimentary, Alex, and said he could sell them! And the catering, well, George's firm just seems to take over.'

'So will you give me carte blanche on the rest?'

'You can't do it by yourself,' she said.

'The guys delivering the piano have worked with me before,' I said. 'They're not cheap, but you only get what you pay for.'

'That doesn't matter,' she said. 'That's the last thing that matters. George has been stomping around bellowing – he's so funny. He keeps waving his cheque book around as if it was a magic wand. I said to him, George, it's who you wave it at. These people are all foreign, Alex, Chinese, I think. I don't know what to wear.'

'Marjorie, you concentrate on clothes and catering,' I said, flicking through my business phone book. 'I'll call you this evening and be over first thing in the morning. You'll see.'

'Bless you, Alex,' she said.

The estate agent was hovering. 'I'll do some working out and call you tomorrow,' she said.

'Hold on,' I said. 'I want to sell really fast. I'm going abroad – just give me a rough idea. I want to drop my keys with you next Wednesday and then I'm off.'

'You'll need to have an idea of price,' she said.

'That's your job,' I said, 'Call me by all means, but it's speed I'm after.'

She looked bemused. 'Up to you,' she said.

'It's very important,' I said. 'It's a whole new life, you see.'

She smiled and promised to do her best.

Then I rang the ferry company, my ears buzzing as they repeated the details back to me once I'd booked – two tickets, North Shields to Norway, 10 am,Wednesday week, Alex Scott and Jodie D'Acosta.

My sweet lord, it felt good to hear our names together in the same breath. Like an affirmation.

I made a list for Marjorie and spent the next three hours spending vast sums of Turner money over the phone. I heard a hellish banging outside – god, the estate agent had taken me at my word and I watched the For Sale sign being nailed into place. It felt real then, like the signature on a long and tortuous letter. *For Sale* drew to a close all my years of lonely hours, and the illusions of warmth I had clutched, making the best of every bad or mediocre situation, sex and alcohol creating a miasma that had passed for happiness. Half-life. The undead.

Goodbye to all that!

I sipped coffee and felt a wrap-around grin take over my entire face. Suddenly I was aching all over, my thighs and arms registering the beautiful love I'd shared with Jodie, my heart thundering with memories and such a sweet and tender certainty. Suddenly everything seemed so right.

I slid into a deep bath and dropped in lavender and bergamot. It was evening now, and there was just one phonecall to make before I'd go to bed and speak with my angel, my love, my forever lover, my Jodie.

My Jodie.

It was bliss to savour those words.

So I rang Marjorie Turner and she said yes to everything, and told me she'd spent the afternoon having a dozen outfits delivered; how could she choose, they were all wonderful, and how early could I be there the next day and help her decide? I knew I wouldn't sleep much, in this strange buzzing space without Jodie, so I said seven and she caught her breath.

'I'm always up at dawn' she said. 'Thank you, Alex. George says I should take nerve tablets – don't you think *he's* got a nerve?'

'Get them' I said, 'and put them in *his* tea.'

She liked that idea.

I lit lime and frankincense candles around my bedroom and got into bed.

And then I leaned on one elbow and rang Jodie, my fingers shaking.

'Darling,' I said, 'my darling.'

'Missed you.'

We said it together.

'What have you been doing?'

Together, again.

'The sign's up,' I said.

'Sign?' she said.

'*For Sale*. Lock, stock and barrel.'

'Is that weird?' she said.

'It's wonderful,' I said, 'and I've booked tickets.'

'Wow,' she said. 'Hey, Alex, do you know that I love you?'

'Yes,' I said, 'and do you know that I love you, Jodie?'

'Yes, I do,' she said. 'Where are you?'

'In bed,' I said, 'with candlelight. Without you. Counting down the sleeps, my love.'

'Me too,' she said. 'I've got the shop covered. And Tim called in, smirking like a gnome. He brought me yellow roses – he said they're the flower of love between women.'

'They are,' I said. 'You have some in your garden.'

'He was funny,' she said. 'He wants to take the credit for being Cupid. Said he wants to hitch-hike on the feeling for a while. You know how clever he is with words? And he wasn't being clever this time. He seemed really sincerely happy for us.'

'He is,' I said. 'Tim believes in love, Jodie. Has he talked to you about Harold?'

'He did today,' she said. 'He says he's going to become an Internet vicar so he can marry us.'

'What did you say?' I asked, my heart fluttering like a bird in a sunlit pool.

'I said I'd have to ask you,' she said, 'so I'm asking you. Alex, will you marry me?'

'Yes,' I said. 'Will you marry me?'

'Yes,' she said.

'Well, that's OK then.'

Together once more.

'Wow,' she said, and I knew her heart was going as wild as mine. 'That feels like – something else.'

'Like changing a gear?' I said. 'Like overdrive?'

'Hang-gliding,' she said. 'That rush when you jump into the air – yes, and Alex, now I'm floating. I can feel you flying with me, in me, god, you're everywhere.'

I cradled the phone as if it were made of eggshell, for she felt so close to me, so precious and near.

Our words caressed the night air and we loved each other to reluctant sleep. Who knows who slept first – I knew we'd fallen through the waves of ecstatic colour, visiting the freedom of infinity and dreams at exactly the same moment.

Thirty-two

Dawn found me driving one-handed through a rosy glow that burned into gold, talking to Jodie as I beat my way to the Turner estate. Talking to Jodie all the way up the drive, tearing myself away only as Marjorie opened the front door. She was wearing a designer track suit and slippers, her hair off her face in a white Alice band, and I thought how comfortable she seemed compared with the last time.

'Alex,' she said, 'how can you look so good first thing? You look like – well, as if you've been on a health farm. You must tell me your secret.'

Love, Marjorie, love minus zero – no limits.

'I had a good night's sleep,' I lied. 'Always sets me up.'

'I've asked George to send some of his chaps over,' she said. 'They're very strong and there's so much to do! And I've got several ladies lined up for cleaning.'

'You're brilliant,' I said, 'and let's do coffee. In the garden, Marjorie – would you like that?'

'Well, I'll have tea,' she said, 'but definitely the garden.'

Sitting next to the azaleas and palm trees in the sunshine recalled my Jodie and the last two glorious mornings – six sleeps until we were really, truly together! I spread my papers out on the *faux* rustic table and jotted a timetable for the next three days. I prayed that the sunshine would continue.

It was 8 when George's men arrived, seven of them, built like wrestlers, Jo as their gaffer, and it was 8.30 by the time they'd emptied the living room onto the wide patio. They turned themselves into painters then, simply by adding white overalls. I scrawled the colours on each wall and Jo said *right you are* as the sound of Radio One filtered into the peaceful garden, meaning work. Marjorie's ladies flew in to purge and polish.

And then the vans started to arrive. Some angel was looking after me, for the first one brought the carpets and stacked them in the hall, and the second emptied out a jungle worthy of Kew. Just as I'd asked, they'd colour-tagged the pots, and Marjorie and I supervised her gardener and his two gormless assistants in the swimming pool.

'Trust me,' I said. 'Just about everybody loves Elvis and even those who don't love him know who he is. We'll put a background loop tape on in here – just loud enough to hear, and there are some statues coming that'll just set it off – I know it's kitsch and trashy, Marjorie, but what else would look right?'

I didn't tell her the statues were pink flamingoes, but I knew their gaudiness would add a touch of humour – even the greatest snob walking would see it was tongue-in-cheek.

'I'd never have thought of that,' she said, 'but you're right. We can't exactly hide the pool.'

'If you've got it, flaunt it,' I said.

We had decided to leave the hall just the way it was, just replacing the Gainsborough with George Turner's portrait and adding a Chinese rug twenty feet in diameter. Marjorie wasn't happy though, when the portrait hung in place under the balcony between the elaborate curved staircases.

'It's not me,' she said, 'but George says I should be up there beside him and I hate my portrait.'

'Show me,' I said.

She asked the butler to get it and said she had it hidden in the larder, face to the wall. I could see why she didn't like it, although the likeness was excellent. Where George looked like a well-to-do mayor, she looked almost regal, in green satin, diamonds and pearls.

'Let's see,' I said, and the shifty-looking butler helped me place both portraits. I switched on the magnificent chandelier and took Marjorie outside.

'Forget it's you,' I said. 'Just see what you think – as if you'd never been in this house before.'

I told her it made it look like a family home and she seemed mollified.

We whisked into the reception room and she gasped – most of the walls were covered and three of George's thugs were screwing scaffolding into place for the ceiling. Jo winked at me.

'Just the fiddly bits, Mrs Turner,' he said. 'I do them myself.'

Marjorie laughed nervously but it was lovely to watch his enormous hands using a pencil-size brush as he worked gold into the swirls of ornate plaster.

And then a pantechnicon arrived, driven by Steven. Tim climbed out of the cab and nodded at me.

'I'm a hitch-hiker,' he said. 'Just too, too curious! My, my, Alex, we can have some fun here!'

I introduced him and Josh and Steven to Marjorie – as my design team. The boys enthused and got Marjorie to give them the grand tour and Tim strolled around indoors with me.

I checked my watch around four. Time to go home and get over to Fleur, which had Tim raising an eyebrow at me.

'Loose ends, Smallboy,' I said. 'I assume you're my house guests?'

'We'll look after ourselves,' he said, 'and meet you here tomorrow?'

'I'll be home tonight,' I said, 'if it's any of your business.'

'Just checking,' he said, then added seriously, 'just don't want you to screw this one up, Alex, and I feel half-responsible for screwing it up last time.'

'I don't screw this one up,' I said. 'It is, always has been and always will be the real thing. My special thing.'

'Thank god,' he said. 'I know I joke, but really, Alex, alone is an awful place to be. Even with memories.'

'Tell me about it,' I said, clasping his hand for a moment.

'Alex, we haven't even looked at my dresses,' Marjorie said.

'Let's do that tomorrow,' said Josh. 'I love dressing people!'

'Don't worry,' I told Marjorie, 'We're right on schedule.'

Thirty-three

It was strange to be driving to see Fleur without having a host of glorious fantasies running through my head about how we could please and tease and drive each other crazy. I felt like a novice in an arcane cult where progress and acceptance depended on my inner worthiness rather than any rules and regulations. As if something beyond human approval had started me on some kind of weird initiation test without there being any pass or fail or judgement other than my own.

Jodie meant love and Fleur was sweet temptation and I have the willpower of an amoeba. But the burning certainty I had about me and Jodie branded through my every cell that I wanted to be something real, something more than just pondlife, and this was my first crucial step out of the primordial slime.

I wondered if the first newt felt like this, daring to stick its waterlogged little nose into dry air, hauling itself through mud on soft and vulnerable evolving lumps of flesh and bone that would become legs on some far-distant day. Whatever drove that newt out into the air, it was too strong to resist. How did it feel when sunshine hit its eyes, so accustomed to the dim swirl and sweep of water? Were there floods of tears as it grew accustomed to the unrelenting daylight? Or did it all happen the way some people say, when a meteorite hit the earth and unbalanced everything, making dry land where there had been ocean, desert where there were forests, arctic wastes where mammoths had grazed on lush grass and hundreds of bright and nameless flowers – and a newt would simply find itself gasping on dry earth. Adapt or die.

Evolution.

I knew that with this Love, with Jodie, it was all of this and more – and just how much more we would find out together.

A revolution for me, true revolution. Which is going all around the world and returning to your starting point to find your true self. And that's revelation. Oh boy.

I was three streets away from Fleur and I pulled over and parked, needing to smoke and wanting to talk to Jodie and feeling it wasn't OK somehow for how could I tell her I was about to have dinner with someone else, someone I'd been wildly and sluttishly and unashamedly intimate with. Hey, what if she had loose ends like this to tie up as well? Would I want to know? Would I be bothered?

No, I wouldn't want to know and if I did, yes, I'd be bothered, and that would be just in case...I realised that the thought of Jodie making love with someone else *now* would be unbearable. Whatever she had done between that crazy runaway time and when we held each other again was *then* and nothing to do with me at all. Just hoped she hadn't been hurt with any of it.

So I rang her and told her answerphone I loved her and hoped whatever she was doing was making her happy, and I told her it was only four sleeps until our boat carried us away to forever.

Fleur was office-immaculate when she opened the door, a well-cut navy suit, cream blouse and shoes in both colours. Her hair was clipped back and she air-kissed my cheek. I followed her into her kitchen, wondering if her sixth sense had told her that I had changed.

'Drink, darling?' she said, 'I'm doing G & T.'

'Sounds good to me,' I said and smiled at the brisk sloosh of gin and clink of ice cubes in a wave of tonic.

'Cheers,' she said, her glass touching mine. But her eyes didn't come anywhere near me, and looked a little pink.

'Fleur,' I said, 'something's wrong. Just tell me. I've got things to tell you too, my sweet. Shall we just say whatever it is?'

'We could,' she said. 'I feel rather dramatic and can't find playful, Alex. Maybe we should tell what there is to tell and then decide what to do with this evening. Oh god, you look very relaxed, damn you.'

'Someone's got to do it,' I said, thinking of Jodie standing beside me, my inspiration, my battlecry.

'Let's have a fresh drink,' Fleur said. 'I'm two ahead of you anyway. Let's sit down.'

We sat for a moment and she wiped her nose.

'You go first,' she said. 'Let me be a coward. Be a gent, dear Alex, and just spit it out. Can't be worse than mine. I mean it. We always said we'd be honest. So you first. I insist and I promise you I'll be honest too.'

She lit a cigarette and tried to smile, muttering something about hay fever.

'OK,' I said, taking a fizzing gulp of my drink. 'Here goes. Fleur, I'm in love. It's serious and if it isn't the real thing then there isn't one.'

She stared at me, her eyes blazing. 'What?' she screamed, and her glass flew past my ear and shattered against the wall. She flew at me and hit my shoulders and wrenched at my jacket. Jesus!

'Fleur, for chrissake,' I said, holding her wrists.

Suddenly she was laughing, uncontrollable mirth shaking her body as she kicked her shoes off and patted my arm, hysterical. She tore the clip from her hair and shucked her jacket onto the floor.

'It's OK,' she said. 'Girl, you know how to surprise a girl. Bloody hell.'

'Are we in for a bumpy night?' I said.

'Another drink,' she said, 'and then I'll tell you mine.'

Whether her laughter was real or damn good acting, it felt better.

'You bastard, Alex,' she said. 'You're not, but you have rather stolen my little thunder.'

'Thunder on,' I said.

'I'm getting married,' she said, flourishing the third finger of her left hand with its platinum and diamond ring.

I choked on my drink. 'Bloody hell, too,' I said. 'Sort of leaves me speechless.'

'I suppose we could say it's rather sudden,' she said, and clasped my hand.

'Well, congratulations, Ms O'Brien,' I said and chinked my glass against hers. I felt a bubble of joy rise through my whole body from my toes to my head.

'And congratulations too,' she said. 'Has that Emilia finally seen sense?'

'Emilia who?' I said. 'Don't contaminate an evening with that name. No. It's not her. Never was, only I was too much of a fool to see it.'

'And it can't be Chris,' Fleur said, 'although she is rather a catalyst, Alex.'

'Catalyst? How?'

'Well, dear heart,' Fleur said, playing with her ring, 'I did have a little play with Chris since you were away and suddenly I thought, god, that's me if I don't do something about it. I mean, Alex, I know age doesn't matter, but it has to me for the last few years. Hence the beauty torture every morning. Terrified of being old! And I will admit to hovering around my half-century, but Chris is hovering way ahead of me. Doesn't look it, but there's a jaded feel to her. And I know we drink, darling, but she drinks too much and too often. Nothing moral, but drinking like that makes one querulous and tedious and then there's this awful control thing she's got. Frightening.'

'So you found a fiancé instead?' I said, 'Pretty smart in a few days, Fleur.'

She smiled and looked away and her eyes were glowing when she looked at me.

'And you don't mind that he's a chap?'

'Fleur! So long as he's nice and good for you. I don't think hes and shes, I think people. I mean it's always been women for me, but I did try to be straight once, you know. If I fell in love with a guy then I'd be happy for the love and to hell with the gender. Tell me about your chap – what's his name? Come on, Miss Priss, spill.'

Fleur wouldn't say more until we ate and wouldn't shift. We decided to go out for dinner and she changed from her office mufti into a wheat-coloured shift scattered with pale green flowers.

'Thai,' she said, and rang for a cab.

With a dozen eggshell bowls of fire and spice between us, we relaxed and, looking at her, I knew I liked this woman. Crazy and wilful, what you saw was what you got with Fleur.

And then my phone rang. I was about to switch it off when I recognised Jodie's number. Fleur busied herself with sambal.

'Darling,' Jodie said, 'I missed you, where are you?'

'Having dinner with a friend,' I said. 'She's getting married, so I guess this is a celebration.'

'Were you OK when you rang?' she asked. 'Your voice sounded not quite right.'

'Just missing you,' I said.

'Not long,' she said. 'I won't keep you, my angel.'

'You'd better,' I said.

'Have you told your friend that you're getting married, too?' she asked.

'Can't get a word in,' I said. 'Hey Fleur, I'm getting married too, you know.'

'Wonderful,' she said, 'Congratulations.'

'Let me say hello,' Jodie said. 'I want to know your friends.'

I heard Fleur congratulating my Jodie, then saying yes, she's very special, and I knew she meant me. And then she told Jodie she was very lucky and then I took the phone back and told Jodie we'd talk later. And how very much I loved her.

'Alex,' Fleur said, 'she sounds marvellous. What a beautiful voice. And full of love for you. I'm so glad. So tell me about her.'

So I did, and Fleur nodded.

'There's always been a guard on your eyes, Alex,' she said. 'It added to the air of mystery, but it's gone now. Your eyes are wide open and it suits you.'

'Tell me about Mr Fleur,' I said.

'Girl,' she said, 'his name is Henry and you're not to laugh. He's a very decent chap and I had an affair with him – not twenty years ago, more like fifteen. He couldn't or wouldn't leave his wife and I moved away because it didn't feel right. He left his wife three years later –well, she left him. He contacted me and I was a bitch to him. I was in my single-career-girl phase and had quite a nice decorative fellow at the time. Henry said he'd be there forever for me and every time he's moved he's let me know where he was.'

She paused and toyed with her wineglass.

'So I left Chris very early the other morning,' she said. 'She had a stinking hangover and I was just – bored. I was driving back here when I suddenly thought I didn't want to go to the office or go home, so I just parked up and had a ciggie and did some thinking. You weren't around, you see, and I had come to rather rely on our – interludes – and I suppose I had a bit of a weep and *what's it all about*. I was rooting in my bag for Kleenex and there was my address book. I hadn't put Henry's address in it, just had a loose card and it fell out. I know you go for all that *no such thing as coincidence stuff*, so I rang him – didn't speak, withheld my number and so on, but he answered.'

'And has he got a marvellous voice?' I asked her.

'Not especially,' she said. 'It's a nice enough voice. Anyway, I checked my map and decided to ring in sick to the office and headed off down the road.'

'Where does he live?'

'Cumbria,' she said. 'It took me about four hours and then he was out. So I wandered around and, god, Alex, it was amazing. Hills and trees and a stream and a little cascade of water and a garden that just sort of blends in with the fields. I sat down by a tree in his garden and thought about going off and finding coffee, even breaking in, but then I thought there's probably a Mrs Henry and I'm intruding. But it was so peaceful and I was exhausted so I had a little zizz, and woke up and Henry was just sitting there, smiling at me. We started talking as if it was the most natural thing in the world and now I've resigned and I'm moving over there at the weekend.'

'Well, ain't that romantic?' I said, smiling.

'Not really,' she said, 'but it's safe and good and it's what I want. And what he wants too. I don't think either of us is head over heels, darling, but it's like giving a chance to what might have been if we'd both been free when we first met. Not like your Jodie, Alex – your eyes have got a sparkle I've never even seen there before. Not even after Perrier Jouet.'

We sat quiet for a while and ate and smiled from time to time. I drank sparkling water and felt good and easy right from the inside. Whatever this evening had been in the process of initiation, I felt peace.

Fleur and I hugged goodbye and kissed each other on the cheek. I would be going home that night and talking to Jodie with nothing to withhold or confess and it felt good.

Thirty-four

All was chaos at Mrs Turner's the next day. As if some *enfant terrible* had upended a dozen jigsaw boxes all over the floor and hidden the box lids. I enjoy jigsaws. I knew all the pieces were there and Marjorie didn't, but Tim had worked with me before and just smirked and tugged an invisible forelock.

'Madame *Gauleiter* has arrived,' he said to Steven and Josh, 'and she has a boat to catch, so we'd better hop to it.'

'Once the marquees are up I can relax,' I said, 'and we're doing balloon trees, Tim – did I say that I've claimed them as original?'

'My lippy is super glue,' he said. 'All designers are plagiarists and whores, darling – it's the name of the game. I shall take it as some obscure sort of compliment. But I insist on pink footprints.'

'Naturally,' I said.

Balloon trees are a Smallboy creation and, like all great ideas, very simple and much imitated. They are branches painted luminous or sprayed gold or silver, scattered wherever people will walk. You step on a concealed footplate which releases helium into however many balloons are fixed there and they inflate so the whole thing hovers a little above the ground for about twelve hours. Once people have realised there is a footplate they go looking for others and the whole effect is that of treasure-seeking magic at a children's party. We demonstrated one to Marjorie and she was delighted – worried that the Chinese might find it frivolous but Steven assured her that the colours would enhance her final choice of dress and she relaxed and smiled.

'And of course you must come,' she said, 'all of you!'

'We'd be delighted,' Tim said.

'I'm afraid I won't be able to, Marjorie,' I said. 'I have some very important business in Norway.'

It felt wonderful making that statement. No business had ever been more important.

'We'll take photos,' Tim said, 'for your rather swanky portfolio, Ms Scott. And for mine.'

'Give me five,' I said.

'I'll give you ten,' he said, both hands clasping mine. 'You have a positive glow, dear Alex, an almost ethereal light radiates from you. Angelic, my dear, and that can only come from a pure heart In Love.'

Josh and Steven were gilding huge cut-out Chinese symbols – health, prosperity, long life, hope, unity, freedom, wisdom, peace – and love. These were to float on the lake and catch the sun through the afternoon and then be silhouetted at night by flares and fireworks.

By nightfall we were exhausted, and every hour of the next day would be needed to rehearse and find any glitches or hitches. Marjorie offered us dinner, but tacitly we knew we needed a break from her twittering and worry.

We went to an Indian restaurant that evening, almost too tired to eat. Tim insisted on red wine and swore it was packed with trace minerals. Whatever, it hit the spot and by the time we got back to my flat, I was ready to run through the checklist for the Turner extravaganza.

Marquees, balloons, gold and red metallic confetti, music, boardwalks, floats, fire-eaters, fireworks, scarlet and gold tulle to dress the dining chairs, ribbons ditto to dress the balustrades, orchids, roses and lilies for every alcove and table, eucalyptus, delphiniums, stocks, foxgloves and fern for the huge flower displays in the hall. Outdoor candles in spice, lavender, cypress and vanilla. Indoor in lime, satsuma, orange, tangerine and cinnamon.

Josh and Steven went to bed and I rang Jodie. When I came back downstairs, Tim was sitting looking thoughtful so I joined him for a while with a brandy.

'This will assure your work for the next decade, darling,' he said. 'If you ever come back, that is. And how is the divine Ms D'Acosta?'

'Divine,' I said. 'Just about packed and ready.'

'And you, darling,' Tim asked. 'Are you packed and ready?'

'Ready,' I said, 'haven't packed a thing. If I packed now I'd want to be gone now. That's tomorrow, Tim. But ready? God, am I ever ready.'

'I wanted to say I'm sorry,' he said. 'I feel I screwed things up for you years ago, only she seemed so uncertain and you were so sad. Then she was just so pregnant and you always sounded like you were having a good time. I lost touch with her for a couple of years you know, and we were never really close, Jodie and I. But I am sorry if I could have made it easier or sooner.'

'That's OK, Tim, I said, 'and even if it wasn't, well, it's the past. I'm only interested in now. Which wouldn't be now without your god-awful dinner party.'

'Call me Cupid,' he said. 'We'll have all this done by tomorrow night and I am more than happy to emcee the entire burlesque – that seems to be the role allocated to me if only by default.'

'I was going to ask,' I said. 'I didn't just assume, you know.'

'Baby, I've had my wedding and marriage and funeral,' he said. 'It's your turn now. Sweet dreams.'

I could feel tears on his cheek when I hugged him goodnight, but for all that he was smiling.

Thirty-five

3 am and I was sitting on one of these metal, string-vest effect benches on the litter-strewn concourse of the station. Jodie's last job was to go to London and tell Alice what she was going to do. Then she was taking the milk train. I would meet her at 4.30 and then we'd go the ferry. I said I'd pick her up in London, but she said that was crazy, and while me being crazy was one of my best features, she didn't need me to be exhausted as well. She had plans for me which would need every bit of energy I had. I love it when my whole body smiles and that's the way Jodie always makes me feel.

So why 3 am? Well, I couldn't have slept, anyway. And maybe trains come early and I would not have my darling hanging about among the derelicts and drunks of a late-night-early-morning city.

I rang her at four, three coffees later.

'Darling,' she said and then the phone cut off and fifteen minutes later a text came through from her, cursing the patchy signal on the train.

Then I rang her and her voice was salvation in the night and we talked and the train came in as we were talking and I watched her come out of the door shining like a light, with a case and a bag. We talked as our eyes met in the day-for-night chill of the station and we kept talking until we were right in front of each other and switched off both our phones, knowing we wouldn't need them ever again.

We held each other and then found my car and I drove one-handed through the dawn and she kissed my neck and clasped my hand against her beautiful thigh as I drove. And we stopped and made love in a lay-by, and then in another lay-by.

Breakfast time, we were holding hands in the dockside café, dunking croissants in mugs of coffee, our knees smooching under the table. Jodie said Alice was fine about us and had wanted to come to meet me, but she wouldn't let her. Not now.

Then we were in our cabin and the engines started as we held each other, head-to-toe naked and kissed while the horn sounded and neon galaxies sang in her eyes. And while the boat surged out of harbour and into the open sea, we made love like it was the first time, just like it always was with Jodie.

Always the first time, in all ways the best time.

Our time.

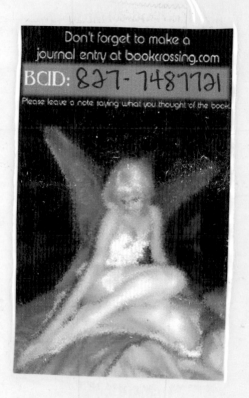

Don't forget to make a
journal entry at bookcrossing.com
BCID: 827-7481721
Please leave a note saying what you thought of the book.

New erotic fiction from Red Hot Diva

Cherry
Charlotte Cooper

It's sexy. It's sassy. It's so, so slutty.

Desperate to pop her lesbian cherry, Ramona soon finds that shagging women in real life bears little resemblance to the dirty books she's been reading under the covers. Every dyke has to ditch the theory and put herself out there if she wants to get some action and *Cherry* goes all the way... Ramona pursues and is pursued by the coolest, hottest, richest, wildest – and sometimes the saddest – girls around.

RRP £8.99 UK/ $13.95 US
ISBN 1-873741-73-1

Scarlet Thirst
Crin Claxton

Lesbian vampires on the prowl!

Sexy Rani is initiated into the vampire lifestyle by the butch dyke Rob and embarks on a hedonistic trip through a sex-fuelled underworld, seducing and being seduced by more and more women who live the Life...

For once, the lesbian vampire story is not just a metaphor: this novel is as upfront about sex as it is about biting into beautiful young necks. They're butch, they're femme, they're out for blood.

RRP £8.99 UK/ $13.95 US
ISBN 1-873741-74-X

The Fox Tales
Astrid Fox

Bizarre. Perverse. Moving.

The dazzlingly filthy erotica of _The Fox Tales_ spans the gamut from sacrilege to Scandinavian myth, from prison dykes to Victoriana, from smug straight boys to mermaids to the devil herself.

These are eighteen of the best of Astrid Fox's sleazy stories, including favourites from previous anthologies and brand new fantasies. Pandering to every taste, her work combines unapologetic West Coast lust with the darker tones of Angela Carter-style magic realism.

RRP £8.99 UK/ $13.95 US
ISBN 1-873741-79-0

The Escort
Kay Vale

Kinky power games, romance and sex, sex, sex

Our heroine is a "tart with an art" – she satisfies scores of women as a high-class lesbian prostitute and pumps the profits into her real passion – designing opulent jewellery.

Enter Naomi, a spoiled princess who buys a night with Harriet and works her way into her affections. But Harriet has a jealous girlfriend – a sexy police sergeant who's not afraid to use the cuffs...

RRP £8.99 UK/ $13.95 US
ISBN 1-873741-84-7

Peculiar Passions
or, The Treasure of Mermaid Island
Ruby Vise

Fun, saucy sex and rip-roaring adventure

Aboard a pirate ship in 1670, runaway Elizabeth meets Jack, who has been disguised as a boy from birth. They both wear lockets that together form the map of a treasure island. They join forces and find themselves...

... battling the pirates for treasure; solving an ancient lusty mystery; performing amazing feats of derring-do; discovering the delights of some serious Sapphic pleasure.

RRP £8.99 UK/ $13.95 US
ISBN 1-873741-83-9

Starburst
Tanya Dolan

Trashy, decadent and compelling – Jackie Collins for dykes!

Seeking fame in London, 18-year-old actress Paula Monroe daringly gatecrashes a showbiz bash thrown by her screen idol, the luscious Karen Cayson. Success may prove elusive, and Paula quickly discovers that her country-fresh teen persona makes glamorous women eager to make love to her - including a dark-eyed, smouldering journalist by the name of Cheryl Valenta. But who can Paula trust, and what is the price of fame?

RRP £8.99 UK/ $13.95 US
ISBN 1-873741-90-1

How to order your new Red Hot Diva books

Red Hot Diva books are available from bookshops including Borders, Libertas!, Silver Moon at Foyles, Gay's the Word and Prowler Stores, or direct from Diva's mail order service on the net at www.divamag.co.uk or on freephone 0800 45 45 66 (international: +44 20 8340 8644).

Please add P&P (single item £1.75, two or more £3.45, all overseas £5) and quote the following codes: Starburst STA 901, Peculiar Passions PEC839, The Escort ESC847, Scarlet Thirst SCA74X, The Fox Tales FOX790, Cherry CHE731.